A massive truck rammed the passenger side of Jackson's SUV...

Bailey's body jerked from the impact. Her seat belt held her in place like a vise. The SUV spun around in a circle like on an amusement park ride. When it finally stopped, they faced the edge of the road and a deep plunge.

"He's backing up to hit us again." Jackson tried to start the car, but the engine began smoking.

The truck rammed into their back bumper, shoving them over the edge. The front end of the SUV tipped in the direction of the drop-off. Bailey stared at the boulders below and gasped.

"Hold on!" Jackson warned.

The SUV's tires hit the ground, and they rolled down the hill faster and faster. Bailey pressed farther back in her seat, her entire body tensing. "Brake! Brake!"

"I'm trying!" Jackson shifted into low gear, then pulled on the emergency brake lever, but nothing slowed their descent...

Tina Wheeler is a retired teacher and award-winning author. She enjoys spending time with her large extended family, brainstorming with writing friends, discovering new restaurants and traveling with her husband. Although she grew up near a desert in Arizona, her favorite place to plot a new story is on a balcony overlooking the ocean.

Books by Tina Wheeler

Love Inspired Suspense

Ranch Under Fire

Visit the Author Profile page at LoveInspired.com.

RANCH UNDER FIRE

TINA WHEELER

LOVE INSPIRED SUSPENSE
INSPIRATIONAL ROMANCE

LOVE INSPIRED SUSPENSE

INSPIRATIONAL ROMANCE

Recycling programs
for this product may
not exist in your area.

ISBN-13: 978-1-335-58755-8

Ranch Under Fire

Copyright © 2023 by Tina McCright

For questions and comments about the quality of this book, please contact us
at CustomerService@Harlequin.com.

Love Inspired
22 Adelaide St. West, 41st Floor
Toronto, Ontario M5H 4E3, Canada
www.LoveInspired.com

Printed in U.S.A.

I can do all things through Christ
which strengtheneth me.
—*Philippians* 4:13

To my husband, the Irish Charmer,
for encouraging me every step of the way.

Acknowledgments

Special thanks to my editor, Dina Davis,
and my agent, Tamela Hancock Murray,
for believing in me and my story.

ONE

Bailey Scott glanced at the time on her cell phone and groaned. She was running ten minutes late. One obstacle after another had fallen in her path that morning. First, her alarm clock quit working at midnight, so she'd overslept. Next, she'd spilled orange juice down the front of her blouse and had to change. Then her neighbor had shown up unexpectedly, needing to borrow coffee beans, and wouldn't stop chatting. Bailey tried in vain to shake off the odd sensation she wasn't supposed to go to work today.

She shifted her heavy purse out of the way, snatched the bakery box off her car's back seat and pushed the door closed with a practiced hip move. The Arizona sun blazed overhead, beating down on her as she rushed through the medical complex's mostly empty parking lot toward the surgical office where she had worked as a bookkeeper for the past ten years. It would be another hundred-degree July day in the small tourist city of Sedona.

Once inside the waiting room, she strode down the aisle formed by cushioned black chairs, her sandals slapping on the tile floor. Amy, their Saturday receptionist, greeted her with a bright smile.

Bailey glanced over her shoulder toward the hall and whispered, "Has Dr. Daniels asked for me yet?"

"Not a word, and I wouldn't go back there looking for him. He said he didn't want to be disturbed until his first appointment." The landline rang. Amy lifted a purple-painted fingernail to indicate she would get back to Bailey in a minute. "Red Rock Cosmetic Surgery." Pause. "Yes, the doctor is in. Can I book an appointment for you?" The petite college student furrowed her brow and dropped the receiver back in its cradle. "How rude!"

"What was rude?" Bailey opened the box of sugary treats in Amy's direction. The mouth-watering aroma wafted through the air, reminding Bailey that she needed more than coffee and a sip of orange juice to start her day.

"The guy hung up on me," Amy complained as she reached for a chocolate doughnut with sprinkles. "Remember when Dr. Daniels's ex-wife served him with divorce papers? Maybe the caller was another process server tracking him down. It would explain why the doctor is in such a mood."

"I don't think so. The divorce finalized last month, so that should all be done with," Bailey pointed out. "And no patients have threatened to sue since that woman two years ago who got mad that she didn't end up looking like Jennifer Aniston." Bailey chose a cinnamon roll and closed the box.

The young blonde shrugged. "We'll find out soon enough."

"Let's hope for an uneventful day, for all our sakes." On the way to her office, Bailey glanced at her employer's closed door at the end of the hall. Her heart ached as she remembered the long, agonizing divorce

Dr. Daniels had never wanted. She made a mental note to keep him in her prayers, placed her cell phone on her tidy oak desk and stashed her purse away in the bottom drawer. One glance at the computer printer reminded her she had planned to replace the toner cartridge this morning. She took a huge bite of her cinnamon roll, licked the frosting from her lips and headed back down the hall.

Amy was answering another call when Bailey passed by the waiting room on her way to the walk-in supply closet. She stepped inside the small space and scanned the floor-to-ceiling shelves for the box she needed.

"Where's the doctor?" demanded an unfamiliar deep voice coming from the reception area.

"Is he expecting…" Amy's voice faltered.

"I'll find him myself."

Bailey turned to march out of the closet and deal with the pushy man. She froze at the sound of a shrill scream, two nerve-wracking blasts and a loud crash. *Gunshots! Those were gunshots!* Fear clutched her chest, making it hard to breathe. *Amy! Please be okay. God, please help her. Please help all of us.*

Sweat beaded on Bailey's forehead, and her palms turned clammy. She drew in tiny gasps of air to keep from fainting.

Hide.

The single word popped into her mind. Shaking, she forced her hand to reach for the doorknob. With her heart pounding in her ears, she eased the door shut and pressed her finger against the knob's push-button lock. Darkness enveloped her, but she knew God stood with her.

Through the door, she could hear Dr. Daniels yell, "Amy! What happened?"

No! Go back to your office. Bailey's gut reaction was to warn the doctor, but the sound of heavy footsteps in the hall preempted her. She couldn't move. Couldn't think. The temperature in the cramped room spiked— or at least, it felt that way.

"There you are, Daniels," the intruder growled. "We need to have a little talk about—"

"Amy!" the doctor yelled, his voice filled with alarm. "What did you do to her?"

Bailey held her breath, waiting for the response. She'd never been so afraid in all her life.

"Don't worry. The chick didn't feel a thing."

Amy... Bailey choked up, and tears slid down her cheeks.

"What do you want?" The doctor sounded braver than Bailey would have expected under the circumstances. *Does he know this guy?*

"For starters, where's your nurse?"

Nurse? Was he just guessing that a doctor would have to have a nurse working for him, or was he actually looking for Stephanie? *If so, he's about a week late*, Bailey thought. Stephanie had quit only days earlier, telling them that her husband had gotten a great last-minute job opportunity in Hawaii.

"She doesn't work for us any longer."

"Anyone else here?"

Bailey's pulse skipped a beat.

"No."

"Then take me to your office."

This could be her chance to sneak out without being seen. It would be safer to stay put...but Bailey knew she could never live with herself if she didn't try to get help. She silently waited for the footsteps to fade away and then inched open the door. With a glance to her right, she watched the shooter disappear into the doctor's office down the hall. A ski mask hid his features.

The back door was six feet to Bailey's left. Her legs trembled, but she pressed on with quiet, deliberate steps.

"You idiot!" The shooter's voice cracked with anger, and sounds of a struggle ensued.

Two more gunshots were fired. Bailey's flight instincts hijacked her self-control. She raced to the door and shoved her hands against the horizontal metal bar to release the lock. The loud metallic clack announced her departure as she bolted outside.

She sprinted down the alley, mind racing as she tried to figure out where she could go. All the other medical offices around her were closed for the weekend. There was nowhere to take shelter. How could she escape from a gunman?

She had nothing to help her. No purse. No phone. No car keys. Traffic hummed around the little shopping center located half a block away. If she could get there before the gunman caught up with her, then she could find a store and call for help.

But that was a big "if."

A black SUV with tinted windows entered the lot and drove straight toward her. Was the driver another bad guy? How could she tell? Trying to play it safe, she dashed toward the nearest tree that might provide some protection from oncoming bullets.

The SUV's window rolled down, and a man with light brown hair and a cowboy hat leaned his head out. "Bailey! What's wrong?"

It took her mind a second to recognize the concerned voice. *Jackson.* The handyman the management company had recently hired. *Thank You, Lord.* Before she could tell him that she needed his help, she heard the crunch of gravel and turned to see the masked gunman emerge from the corner of the building with his weapon raised.

Her knees threatened to buckle.

Jackson's gaze followed hers, and his eyes widened. "Get in!"

The click of car locks propelled her to yank open the back door and dive inside.

"Hold on!" Bullets pelted the side of Jackson's SUV. He floored the gas pedal, causing them to lunge forward.

Terror filled her. Her dive across the back seat had come up short. The bottom half of her legs stuck out the open door, and her grip on the middle-seat cushion kept slipping. Any second now, she might fall out and find the gunman standing over her.

She groped around until she felt the seat belt strap, then tugged it closer and hung on with both hands. The door swung back and forth, hitting her calves as the handyman careened around a lamppost and sped away, with gunfire chasing after them.

Jackson Walker flew out of the parking lot and swerved into oncoming traffic. Angry drivers slammed on their brakes and honked their horns. He ignored the gridlock he'd caused behind them and sped down the street. Fleeing a gunman went against his instincts. He wanted to stay and fight but couldn't put Bailey's life at even greater risk.

He glanced over his shoulder to where she hid, sprawled

out over the back seat, facedown, clinging to a seat belt strap. "You okay?"

"Yes. No." She shook her head repeatedly. "He shot Amy! And your door isn't shut all the way."

"Yeah, I know. Just hang on for now. I don't care what happens to the door. I'll stop when we're safe." He'd heard the door rattle back and forth a couple of times but couldn't do anything about it with a masked man firing at them. He could see Bailey in the rearview mirror, her knees bent and feet in the air, trying to keep her legs inside the vehicle. His pulse quickened. If she fell out into this traffic, she'd end up in the hospital, if not the morgue.

"You need to call the police!" she shouted. "Amy and Dr. Daniels could be bleeding to death."

Before he could answer, a souped-up green muscle car revved its engine three car lengths behind them. Jackson changed lanes. The other driver followed his lead and then slid into place behind them, close enough for Jackson to see he wasn't the shooter. The masked man had been thin and wore all black. The driver behind them wore white and had wide shoulders.

"I think we have a tail," he warned.

"Do something!" Bailey pleaded.

"I am." The yellow light up ahead turned red, and Jackson sped through the intersection. Unrelenting, the other car chased after them, dodging oncoming cross traffic and their chorus of honking horns.

Jackson raced toward the next light but changed his mind when he glanced in the rearview mirror and spotted the gun hanging outside the green car's window. He made a sharp left at the last second. Their pursuer slammed on his brakes a moment too late, missing the turn. Tires squealed, and the weekend traffic boxed him in.

"What's happening?" Bailey's voice shook. "I can't see anything. Did you lose him?"

"Not for long."

An incoming call displayed his brother's name on the dash screen. He pressed the button to accept the call. "Cole, you're on speaker," he said, as a way of warning the detective not to divulge any confidential information.

"Shots were fired at the medical complex where you work." Cole's authoritative tone filled the SUV. "Where are you?"

"Trying to shake a tail." Jackson checked his rear-view mirror and glanced down each side street, keeping an eye out for more trouble. "The receptionist and doctor at Red Rock Cosmetic Surgery have probably both been shot. I have a witness with me."

"Send an ambulance!" Bailey pleaded from the back seat. "Maybe it's not too late for them."

"Who is that?" Cole sounded more surprised than curious.

"Bailey Scott. The surgeon's bookkeeper." Jackson blew through the four-way stop and hung a quick left. "A guy in a ski mask shot up my car trying to get to her. Then a bigger guy in a loud green muscle car tried to take us out. I don't know how many men they have. They'll expect us to head to the police station. We can't risk an interception."

"I hear you. An ambulance is on the way to your office, ma'am," Cole said. "Jackson, we're spread thin, but I'll arrange an escort to a safe location. Can you find a place to hide until I get back to you?"

"Remember where we used to drive quads?"

"That'll work."

There were advantages to having grown up nearby. It meant that he knew the area—knew how to get around, how to go to ground…and how to blend in as he gathered all the necessary information for the DEA.

He hadn't been part of the operation to capture Dante Hill, the kingpin of a massive local drug trafficking ring, but Jackson knew how it had gone down. They'd been right on the verge of making the arrest when the kingpin had fled the country—tipped off only hours before the planned raid by a leak they still hadn't been able to track. A leak they strongly suspected had come from the local police.

The case had stalled for months, but finally they'd gotten a new lead. The man's associates had been spotted frequenting a particular dentist's office. Before attempting to arrest the men, the agency group supervisor wanted someone to surveil them, see if their movement would reveal where the kingpin was hiding. But to keep from spooking Hill's goons, they needed someone who could operate on-site without drawing any attention.

Jackson had grown up on a ranch outside Sedona and had attended high school with the vice president of the medical complex's management company. It had been easy to get a job as the medical complex's new handyman. He had spent the last month taking surveillance pictures and listening through a hidden microphone he'd planted in the dentist's office. He'd been able to positively identify the men, but the investigation had stalled there. He hadn't been able to follow them back to their hideout without drawing their attention, and he also couldn't enlist the help of the local police—besides Cole—since they still hadn't identified the leak.

The situation had been boiling toward a climax for

days, and Jackson wasn't surprised that it had ended in a shooting. But he *was* surprised to find Bailey somehow trapped in the middle of it.

A glance over his shoulder at the frightened woman made him want to comfort her, to assure her that he had the training and experience to keep her safe. But he couldn't do that without blowing his cover. Only his closest family members and best friend knew he was a federal agent. He had to keep it that way. The last time he revealed his undercover status to an innocent woman, she had been murdered after sharing his secret with a friend. He wouldn't allow that to happen again.

Bailey lifted her head off the seat. "Where are we going?"

"Someplace safe." Memories from his youth guided him toward a secluded area. He reduced speed, turned down the alley behind a strip mall and stopped. "You can sit up and close the door now, but make it fast."

With quick, fluid movements, she jerked up, slammed the door shut and then buckled herself in. Black mascara marks streaked her pale face where tears had fallen, and he could see how hard she was struggling to hold herself together.

His jaw tightened. He vowed to catch the men trying to kill her.

Jackson studied the overgrown weeds bordering the asphalt until he located the entrance to their escape route. Another check in the rearview mirror assured him they were still alone. "Hold on tight. We're in for a bumpy ride."

She mumbled something he couldn't hear as he drove out of the alley and onto the path that led through federally protected land. A quarter mile in, he turned onto an unpaved road, kicking up rust-colored dust in their wake as they bounced over the uneven ground.

After traveling around the closest hill, where no one could spot them from the main streets, he pulled over. He shifted into Park, unbuckled his seat belt and turned to reassure her. Facial expressions often said more than words. "You're safe now."

"Are you sure?" Bailey met his gaze with fearful sable-colored eyes. She pushed her long, dark, disheveled hair behind her ears as if self-conscious of her untidy appearance.

"For now. Judging from all the overgrowth, no one has been here in years." In his mind, he could still see a group of boys speeding over the hills without a worry in the world. Those carefree days had since been replaced by the never-ending vicious battle he waged against drug cartels.

"I can't believe this is happening." Bailey pressed her lips together, then released a long breath. "Why would that guy attack Amy? Or Dr. Daniels? They didn't deserve to die." The grief in her eyes made his heart ache.

"I don't know. Did the shooter say anything? Make any demands?"

"Why would he shoot at your car?" She pressed on as if not hearing him. "He didn't need to kill us, too. We couldn't see his face."

"We can give a basic description of his physique," Jackson pointed out gently. "And if you heard his voice, you might be able to identify him."

She shuddered. "That means I won't be safe until they're behind bars. And I didn't even know there was more than one until that other guy started following us. Who knows how many more there could be? How can

I ever be sure they've all been caught? I'll always be looking over my shoulder."

"Cole will figure this all out. And we'll help him." Jackson offered a slight smile.

"Is he a detective?"

"Sedona's one and only. They had two, but the other guy retired and moved to Florida."

She arched a brow. "Why did he call you?"

"Well... I've known him all my life. He's my brother."

"Oh, and he knows where you work."

"Exactly."

"I would be dead if you hadn't come along when you did."

His chest tightened. He would hate to see Bailey harmed in any way. She'd always been so sweet to him, offering him a warm smile whenever they met in passing and bringing him homemade brownies as a thank-you gift after he'd helped her move some heavy boxes. He might have asked her out if he wasn't lying to her about his job and spying on dangerous men next door to her office.

"I'm glad I showed up when I did, too." He noticed her once-ragged breathing had returned to normal. "We have a few minutes before we need to leave. Can you tell me what happened?"

Her complexion paled. "I don't know, exactly. I was in the supply closet when I heard a man insist on seeing Dr. Daniels. Then..." Her voice trailed off, and her gaze fell toward the floor of the SUV.

Instinctively, he wanted to lean over the seat to comfort her, but he had to maintain a professional distance. Instead, he waited for her to continue.

"Amy screamed. And then I heard gunshots." She dabbed at her lashes with the pads of her fingers.

"Is that when you ran?"

She shook her head, and her eyes glistened with unshed tears. "I locked the closet door so that he wouldn't find me. I was a coward."

"No, you weren't. You're braver than most people. You got yourself out of there. That took courage."

"Doctor Daniels didn't hide. He confronted the man. I could hear them talking in the hallway."

Jackson had a feeling he knew how this part of the story ended. "Did the gunman say what he wanted?"

"He asked about the nurse—he wanted to know if anyone else was there. Dr. Daniels said no, and then the man wanted to go to the doctor's office. I don't know why." The tears she'd held back now flowed down her cheeks. "He shot Amy. He admitted it. I wasn't able to check on her, but I… I think she must be dead."

"I'm so sorry. She seemed like a sweet kid." Jackson reached for a spare napkin on the passenger seat and handed it back to her.

A full minute passed before Bailey was composed enough to continue. "I waited to open my door but not long enough. I saw him walk into the doctor's office wearing that black mask."

"Did he see you? Is that why you ran?"

She shook her head. "There were two more shots. That's what scared me into running."

"I don't blame you. I would have run, too, if I were in your shoes."

"Somehow, I doubt it." She tilted her head, studying him this time. "Why were you in the parking lot today? You have Saturdays off."

He worked every day while on assignment, but he couldn't tell her that. "I thought I would tackle a few things on my to-do list."

"I see. I'm thankful you were there to save my life."

"And I'm glad I went in today." Gratitude for doing his job always made him uncomfortable. Especially since he was hiding so much from her—like the fact that her boss might have had some involvement with the drug ring, too. Jackson had nothing tying him directly to Hill, but there was a fair bit of evidence pointing to the dentist, and Jackson had observed some strange interactions between the dentist and Dr. Daniels. He had no doubt that the doctor had been the true target of the day's shooting. Poor Amy had just been in the wrong place at the wrong time—a victim of circumstance. And Bailey would have ended up just the same if she hadn't managed to run.

Jackson turned away to survey the surrounding hills covered in sandstone, catclaw shrubs and prickly pear cacti, searching for any sign of danger. The only movement came from a hawk soaring over the canyon. He checked his watch. A quarter past eleven. They shouldn't stay here much longer. Bailey needed a place to rest.

As if on cue, his phone rang. He pressed the button to connect the call. "Cole, you're on speaker again. What did you find out?"

"The lieutenant thinks a junkie looking for drug samples shot up the office and is now after the bookkeeper because she's a witness. He wants you to take her to the same hotel where you had your high school reunion. An officer is waiting for you in the parking lot. I tried to arrange an escort from your current location, but the lieutenant is afraid a cruiser might inadvertently lead the shooter straight to you."

Jackson recognized the expression on Bailey's face. She needed the answer to one question. "Were there any survivors from the shooting?"

A slight pause hung in the air. "I'm sorry. Both the doctor and the receptionist didn't make it."

Bailey's eyes teared up again.

Jackson disconnected the call and made a feeble attempt at making her feel better, as if that were even possible. "Cole is the best detective in the state. He'll keep you safe. You can count on him."

And on me, Jackson thought but didn't say. She probably wouldn't take much comfort in having a handyman protecting her, and he couldn't tell her the truth about his qualifications. But until this was all resolved and she was safe, she'd have both him and Cole watching her back, no matter what.

TWO

Sitting in the back seat of the SUV, Bailey tried to stay calm despite the anxiety gripping her. She feared the assailant might spot them if they drove onto the city streets. No matter how illogical, she wished they could stay hidden here in the hills, far away from the shooter who had so callously taken Amy's and Dr. Daniels's lives.

If it weren't for Jackson, she'd be dead, too. She studied the cowboy's reflection in the rearview mirror. Weeks ago, she'd first noticed his broad shoulders and rugged features, especially his smoky-blue eyes. Little had she known then, God had a plan when He brought the handyman to the medical complex.

"Do you want me to move up front?" she asked.

"It would be better if you stayed put until we reach the hotel. You're harder to spot back there with the dark window tinting." His overly concerned expression troubled her. She must look worse than she'd thought.

Jackson turned over the engine, and after a moment of silence, he added in a softer tone, "The police department has a social worker who will help you get through this. I've met her before. She's understanding. You'll like her."

Bailey could probably trust his judgment. Jackson seemed like a good man.

She watched the cowboy steer back onto the road. "Jackson?"

"Yes?" He paused for a second to look at her.

"When you showed up in the parking lot, I thanked God for sending you. You could have driven off when the guy raised his gun, but you didn't. I'll never forget how you put yourself in danger. And I will pray for you every day for the rest of my life."

"I'll pray it's a long, happy life." He offered a slight smile, but it quickly faded. Did his momentary appearance of unease have to do with prayer or with God? Or both? Or was she reading too much into nothing?

They drove down the hill slower than they had on the way up, but she still rocked back and forth in her seat as Jackson navigated the rough terrain. Her gaze shifted out the window to their surroundings. Sedona's rust-colored dirt and green vegetation blurred together into a cloudy vision of brown while she tried to think of anything other than the loss of her coworkers.

The SUV bounced over the curb, separating the paved strip mall alley from the undeveloped land. The sounds of nearby traffic grew from a purr to a roar, and her pulse quickened. "I don't think we should go this way. The shooter could be waiting for us."

"The alley leads to a side street. If he's searching for us, he'll be looking on one of the main thoroughfares leading to the police department."

Bailey studied her clasped hands, hating that she'd become a weak, frightened version of her former self. Although never the type to bungee jump or scale the sides of cliffs, she had always prided herself on facing her problems head-on.

Until three years ago. She'd lost her confidence after falling for a man who lied, cheated and stolen from her. That situation had severely shaken her faith in other people. If she allowed the events of this day to make matters worse, she might end up afraid all the time, never able to trust anyone. Her stomach clenched. There had to be something she could do to make her feel in control of her life again. Maybe if she helped Jackson, it would take her mind off her current state of anxiety.

She leaned close to the front seat. "I'll let you know if I see the shooter or anyone else who looks suspicious. Like anyone pointing a gun at us."

With a nod, he answered, "Yell *gun* if you do, and I'll floor the gas pedal."

She nodded, feeling a tiny bit of her confidence coming back. Even if on a small scale. She eased back against the seat and stared out the windows, searching for bad guys.

The phone rang again, and Jackson pushed the button on his dashboard. "Cole, give us good news."

"I wish I could. Where are you?" The detective's tone made Bailey's stomach churn.

"We just left the hill," Jackson answered.

"A green muscle car was spotted near the car wash on the usual route to the hotel. Take the dirt road to the rear parking lot. Use any shortcut you can find. And watch your back."

"That's Bailey's job."

She couldn't help but smile.

After the call ended, Jackson turned right. The two-lane road took them behind a popular Italian restaurant and the resort where she'd once attended a friend's wedding. Only a few cars traveled in their direction, and none of them turned to follow their SUV.

She recognized the golf course coming up on their right. Her former fiancé had played there every Saturday. Just one of many memories of him that she would rather forget. She'd been such a fool. The first time he lied to her, she should have walked away. Why had she given him another chance?

Jackson continued driving to the far end of the course until the only golfers in sight drove their cart back to the clubhouse. Once they disappeared, he made a sharp turn and sped over the grass. "Hold on. Where we want to go is on the other side of the fairway."

Bailey grabbed on to the seat belt strap pulled taut across her lap with one hand and the door handle with the other and braced herself. "Are you sure this is what Cole meant by 'shortcuts'?"

With increasing speed, they approached a mound near a sandbox and took flight. Her stomach jumped to her chest and then fell back into place when they landed. The SUV bounced several times before lunging forward again. She drew in a deep breath, then checked the side mirror. "Are we being chased?"

"Not yet, and I'm trying to keep it that way."

They flew over another mound and jetted toward the gap in the line of bushes bordering the residential street. Branches scraped the sides of the SUV, causing her to cringe at the nails-on-the-chalkboard-type sounds.

She breathed easier once they reached a paved road again.

Jackson continued speeding away even after they

completed another turn. "Still no one following us. So far, so good."

"Have you ever driven over the golf course before?"

"When I was sixteen. Only then it was on a motor-cycle."

Each time he turned his head to make sure the coast was clear, she gazed at his intense expression beneath the brown Stetson and wondered if he raced cars even now when he wasn't maintaining medical-office build-ings. She knew so little about him. But what she knew so far, she liked—not least because his escape-driving stunts were keeping her safe from dangerous felons.

She scanned their surroundings for anyone who looked like they might want to shoot and kill them. All she saw were upscale ranch-style homes sitting on spacious lots with breathtaking views of the towering rock formations in the distance. "How much farther?"

"About three miles. That shortcut shaved five min-utes off our travel time. Every second counts."

She nodded even though he probably wouldn't notice.

Up ahead on her left, a blonde woman driving a lux-ury car full of children backed out of a garage. Bai-ley observed the surreal scene as Jackson drove past them. How could anyone's life look so normal when a shooter had just murdered innocent people a short dis-tance away?

What would her tomorrows look like? Would she have nightmares for the rest of her life? Could she ever work for another surgeon? What would she say during interviews when they asked why she'd left her last po-sition? What if she left the medical field? Would she find another job? Was she a horrible person for wor-

rying about her future when Amy and Dr. Daniels no
longer had theirs?

When Bailey finally escaped the quagmire of her
thoughts, she watched the neighborhood fade away behind them. The dirt road Jackson turned onto appeared
to connect with the other side of town.

"Try to relax," Jackson encouraged. "I haven't seen
anything out of the ordinary."

At that moment, a massive dark truck idling in
a turnoff sped forward and rammed into the back-
passenger side of their SUV. Bailey's body jerked from
the impact. Her seat belt pulled her back against the car
seat and held her in place like a vise. She dug her fists
into her thighs and tried not to scream as they spun
around in a circle. When the SUV finally stopped, they
faced the edge of the road and a deep plunge.

"He's backing up to hit us again." Jackson tried to
start the car, but the engine began smoking. "Hold on!"

This time the truck rammed into their back bumper. Metal screeched as the other vehicle shoved them
over the edge. The front end of the SUV tipped over
the drop-off. Bailey stared at the boulders below and
gasped.

"Hold on!" Jackson warned again.

The SUV's tires hit the ground, and they rolled down
the hill faster and faster. Bailey pressed farther back
in her seat, trying to create more distance between her
and the potentially fatal end of the ride. Her entire body
tensed. "Brake! Brake!"

"I'm trying!" Jackson shifted into low gear, then
pulled on the emergency brake lever, but nothing managed to slow their descent.

The wall of boulders appeared larger and more menacing as the SUV drew closer. Panic consumed her. "We're going to die!"

"Not today." He turned the wheel to the right and drove over a sharp, jagged rock. The front passenger tire punctured, causing the SUV to slump to one side and slow. Not enough to prevent them from hitting the boulders with a loud metallic crunch but enough to make the impact jarring instead of fatal.

Jackson released his seat belt, then turned to rake his gaze over her. "Are you okay?"

"Physically? Yes. Emotionally? No." Bailey's heart pounded in her ears. The image of the masked man appeared in the side mirror. He peered down at them from the road above and raised the gun in his hand. "He's going to shoot us."

"Get down onto the floor." With a tight jaw and narrowed eyes, Jackson grabbed a black pistol from the center console.

Jackson heard the whiz of a bullet right before it hit the passenger-side mirror, sending it flipping through the air and into a bush.

"Stay down," he told Bailey as he sank low and out of sight. He'd glimpsed a safe spot where he could draw the gunfire away from her while minimizing his chances of taking a bullet. "I'm going to sneak behind this boulder next to the car. Don't get up unless I tell you to."

Jackson waited for Bailey to hide before making his move. The driver's-side door resisted his first attempt to open it. He drew in a deep breath, then shoved his shoulder against it, putting all his weight into the effort. The jammed door finally broke loose.

He ignored the pain in his arm as he shifted and

placed one boot outside. The SUV's back window suddenly shattered. Bailey screamed.

Emotion caught in his throat.

"I'm okay," she called out before he could say anything. "Are you?"

"I'm fine." He pulled his leg back in and breathed a sigh of relief. For a moment, he thought she'd been hit.

He shut off his feelings and reverted to work mode.

A second gunshot barely missed their vehicle and ricocheted off a boulder. Jackson glanced over at his side mirror. From the SUV's slanted angle, he could see the shooter step closer to the edge, zeroing in on the perfect shot.

The moment the masked man lifted his weapon, Jackson leaned outside the car and fired. He didn't have quite the angle he wanted, but he hoped the shot would be enough to spook the man out of position. To his relief, their pursuer dove out of sight when he heard the shot.

So now the man knew that he was armed and that they weren't just sitting ducks. But the attacker still had the high ground. Would he keep trying to take a shot? Jackson tried to brace himself for whatever might be coming next…then relaxed with a sigh of relief when he heard a chopping sound, up high and closing in on them. A helicopter.

A door slammed shut, and tires squealed. Jackson lifted his head enough to see the truck's front end back up before it raced away. Through the front window, he watched the helicopter approach their crash scene. Not military or law enforcement, judging by the bright colors. He got back into his seat, turning around to make eye contact with Bailey. "He took off when he heard the helicopter. I guess this guy didn't want a starring role in the evening news. They must have been nearby, covering the shooting at your office."

"News?" Bailey crawled up off the floor and leaned over the front seat to gaze up at the sky through the front window. "I need to use your phone to call my father and let him know I'm all right. He'll be worried sick if he hears about the shooting on TV."

Jackson wished he could grant her request, but this wasn't the time. "I promise we'll get word to your father later. Right now, we need to call for help and hike out of here. We don't know if that guy is gone for good."

Bailey frowned and rubbed the triangular pendant hanging from a silver chain around her neck, but she didn't argue.

He used his cell phone to call his brother. Bailey would only hear his side of the conversation. "Cole, watch what you say," he warned as soon as his brother picked up. "Somebody may have hacked our phones. The shooter from Bailey's office ambushed us. We're fine, but the medical complex's SUV is totaled."

"Where are you?" The pitch of Cole's voice heightened.

"Close to the hotel. The gunman knew to wait for us even though I drove over the golf course to reach the dirt road. No one followed us. Who was in the loop?"

"The lieutenant picked the hotel, and I told him you would enter through the back. The officer assigned to protect Miss Scott once you arrived would have that information as well. Either you're right about our phones being hacked or someone inside the station is feeding the shooter information." Or maybe both scenarios were true. Whoever was passing along information might have planted a bug in Cole's phone.

"Time to switch to burners. But first, we need transportation."

What he really needed was backup—but that wasn't an option. Cole was the only cop that Jackson was completely certain was clean, and they needed him to stay at the station, keeping his ear to the ground. And there were no DEA agents within a hundred miles, even if he was willing to blow his cover by calling them in—which he wasn't.

"Where can I find you?"

"Hawk's mailbox." Hawk was the nickname of a friend who once lived near the dirt road. Jackson ended the call and glanced over at Bailey. Her furrowed brow revealed her trepidation. He could hardly blame her for that—she had a lot to be concerned over. "We'll figure this out, starting with a different place to hide until it's safe for you to go home."

She answered with a nod, but the worry on her face intensified.

The helicopter still hovered high above them. Jackson would need to keep his hat tipped down to shield his face from the evening news. "Time to go."

He stepped out of the wrecked SUV and walked around back to the shattered window to wait for Bailey. When she reached his side, he held out his hand. She glanced up the steep hill and blew out a long breath.

"It won't be so bad," he said. "You'll see."

She hesitated before placing her soft palm in his. Jackson wished he could reassure her by revealing his true profession, but he knew better than to risk his assignment. Or her life. Or his. She'd have to find her comfort elsewhere—maybe in the hymns he used to hear her humming to herself as their paths crossed in the medical complex. He had conducted a background search on everyone in her office after noticing the odd looks exchanged between the plastic surgeon and the dentist, so he knew that she was a churchgoing woman who taught Sunday school. He could only hope her faith brought her comfort through this whole ordeal.

Jackson still believed in God, but his connection to Him had waned as he spent more time surrounded by ruthless criminals. He only attended church services when he stayed at the ranch with his family once a year.

In truth, there was very little in his life that brought him a sense of joy or peace these days. A dozen years ago, working for the DEA had excited him. He'd been eager to tackle new cases, proud of the work he was doing. His enthusiasm had dwindled over the years, but he knew he made a difference. Not everyone could say the same.

The helicopter flew off, and with Bailey's hand in his, he scanned the area to locate a path that wasn't too steep or overgrown. Her sandals, khaki-colored capri pants and short-sleeved yellow blouse were not meant for hiking, but there wasn't anything they could do about that now. He guided her up the hill one step at a time.

The noon sun beat down on them. Beads of sweat on his forehead soaked the rim of his hat. At least their time outside would be limited to no more than five or ten minutes—unless something went wrong.

He glanced up at the clear sky, confirming the rain-like smell came from the creosote bush and not a turn in the weather. Bailey didn't have anything to say as they climbed, making it easier for him to listen for any sign of danger.

All he could hear were the sounds made by her sandals and his boots with each step they hiked over the sand-covered rocks. He guided her off the path to walk around a large shrub, and she lost her footing. Her shriek sent birds flying with a chorus of fluttering wings.

Jackson yanked her up more forcefully than he'd intended. "Are you all right?"

She regained her balance and drew in a calming breath. "Yeah." Looking over her shoulder, she added, "I didn't know that wasn't your car. I hope you don't get in trouble at work."

"They offered it as one of the perks to make up for being on call twenty-four hours a day." He glanced down at the wrecked vehicle and cringed. "The worst thing they'll do is refuse to replace it, but that's not our concern right now. Only thirty more feet to go."

When they reached the top of the hill, he pulled her up over the edge. Suddenly, the sound of crunching gravel alerted him to an oncoming vehicle. There was no place to hide in time if the gunman had returned to finish the job.

THREE

Bailey leaned around Jackson, who shielded her body with his. With her breath caught in her throat, she stared at the bend in the road up ahead. A dark gray truck drove out of the wall of dust permeating the air.

She could feel the tension drop out of Jackson's frame. "It's Cole." Jackson tugged on her hand. "Let's go."

His long stride forced her to hurry to keep up. A pebble wedged between her sandal and foot. She hopped, kicking out the irritant, then rushed to his side. "What were you planning to do if the killer had turned that corner?"

"Tell you to run. Shoot it out."

It sounded like a pretty foolish plan to her. Just because he owned a gun—as many people did in Arizona—didn't make him John Wayne. The surrounding terrain also didn't offer much in the way of protection. What could she do in the middle of a gunfight? Run from bush to bush?

She shook off the hypothetical. Cole was here now, and that was what mattered. Her chances of surviving a battle, if they faced one, had to be greater with a detective than a handyman. Nothing against Jackson, but he'd missed the only shot he took before the helicopter flew overhead. It appeared to her that his strength was evasive driving, even if the condition of the SUV suggested otherwise.

The truck slowed to a stop beside them. Cole rolled down the passenger-side window. "You two all right?"

"Just a few minor bruises and scratches." Jackson tugged open the back door for her.

Bailey's gaze traveled between both men as she scooted over and Jackson climbed inside. The family resemblance was unmistakable. Same strong chin, straight nose and high forehead.

She adjusted her seat belt and noticed the extra-dark tinting on the windows. Was it an official vehicle? "I assume the hotel we were planning to go to is out of the question now that your phones may have been hacked. Are you taking us to a safe house?"

"In a manner of speaking." Cole turned the truck around while he continued, "Our department doesn't own any, but Jackson's apartment isn't registered in his name. It's the safest place for you to lie low for a few hours."

When she looked at Cole in confusion, Jackson explained, "I have a friend who is away on business for a few months. He said I could stay in his apartment."

"Until you find a place of your own?" she asked.

"Something like that." Jackson avoided eye contact with her, and a red flag shot up. What was he hiding?

Back on the hill, she'd felt safe with him. Her heart had even skipped a beat when he'd held her close to protect her. She was grateful for the help he'd given her... and there was no denying that he was a very attractive man. But she couldn't let herself become too drawn to him. His desire to keep secrets reminded her too much of her former fiancé, and she refused to venture down that road again.

"Bailey." Cole's voice jerked her attention toward the front of the truck. "I need to ask you a few questions. I'd usually do this at the station, but, as you heard, we may have a security issue right now." He handed a small device back to Jackson. "We'll record our conversation, and then once it's transcribed, I'll have you sign the printed version."

"Okay." She glanced nervously at Jackson while he pressed a button, then stated the vehicle's occupants, location, date and time.

"Bailey," Cole began, "what happened in the medical complex this morning?"

"A man wearing a ski mask killed innocent people I care about." She told the detective everything she could remember about the hang-up phone call, Amy's screams, hiding in the closet and sounds of a scuffle in Dr. Daniels's office, followed by more gunshots. Then she described the man who followed them in the green car. "The killer was tall and thin," she added, then frowned. "I'm sorry, I know that's not a lot to go on."

"Each piece of information helps." Cole approached every exit off the dirt road with caution. "Bailey, do you have any idea what the shooter wanted?"

Memories of that morning left her feeling drained and heartbroken. "He insisted on going into the doctor's office, but I don't know why." She shook her head in despair. "I wish I had the answers."

Jackson turned off the recorder and met his brother's gaze through the rearview mirror. "She might think of something else once she's had time to rest. If so, I'll let you know."

Cole nodded, and Bailey felt like an unspoken message had passed between the two men.

"Would you do me a favor?" she asked, rubbing the pendant dangling from the necklace her father had given her. "Please call my dad and tell him I'm okay. His name is George Scott, and he lives on Sierra. I'm the only family he has here. And worrying won't be good for his heart condition."

Cole glanced back at his brother again.

Jackson nodded. "Use a burner phone. And don't call while you're at the station."

She found it odd that Cole would look to his brother for permission. He was the detective here, not Jackson.

Once they made it back to the city streets without any altercations, Cole pulled into a fast-food drive-through near an apartment complex. The aroma of french fries permeating the air made her stomach growl. She hadn't thought of eating since she took a bite of her cinnamon roll, which probably still sat on her desk in an office surrounded by yellow police caution tape.

Once they'd gotten their food, Cole drove forward to the parking area and stopped. He passed two bags back to Jackson, who unlocked the door and stepped outside, holding out a hand to help her exit. Bailey didn't know what to think.

"Aren't you coming with us?" she asked when the detective stayed in his seat with his seat belt fastened.

Cole shifted to face her. "I wish I could, but I'm the only detective, which requires me to investigate the crime scene and potential leads. The lieutenant is searching for a better place to hide you. For now, we both agree you're safer with my brother than anyone else."

It didn't take long to put two and two together. "Because a police officer might have told the shooter where to find us."

After a brief pause, Cole reluctantly answered, "It's possible." Then he hastened to reassure her, "But you're in good hands with Jackson. My entire family has had extensive firearms and self-defense training. You can trust him. I'll be back in a few hours."

She took hold of Jackson's outstretched hand and let him pull her from the vehicle. Once again, this cowboy was the only person who stood between her and a gunman.

Jackson surveyed the area with each step they took. At the first set of stairs inside the apartment complex, they climbed up to the second floor. He waited for her on the landing, then escorted her past several doors before unlocking one of them and leading her inside.

She took in the sparsely furnished living room, with its dark brown microfiber sectional and oak coffee table—all screaming bachelor pad. At least the kitchen counters were clean, albeit bare except for a simple white toaster.

"Home sweet home. It's not much," he admitted. "But it will do, for now."

Since they planned to eat, she headed over to the round dining room table and sat in one of the four wooden chairs. "I assume you have furniture of your own somewhere."

"I do, but not here in Sedona. This isn't a permanent move." He rested his gun on the chair next to his, making her feel both safe and uncomfortable. He then unpacked the bags, placing a cheeseburger and fries in front of her. "I had some time on my hands until my next assignment started. The job at the medical complex keeps me busy and brings in extra cash."

"'Assignment'?"

He hesitated. "My bosses own buildings all over the country. I've lived in three different states over the past two years. I have no clue where I'll be this time next year." He didn't sound like he was lying, exactly...but she got the feeling he wasn't telling her the full truth, either.

"That explains why you mostly keep to yourself at work."

"I'm a private person." He walked over to the refrigerator and removed four water bottles. "If you moved as much as I do, you might not feel the need to open up with people you'll only speak to a few times, either."

He had a point, she supposed. Not that she could really imagine choosing that kind of lifestyle. She liked feeling settled. And with her close relationship with her father, she couldn't imagine ever leaving him to work anywhere far from Sedona. Her mother had run off with another man a week before Bailey's second birthday, and her father had raised her by himself. Now it was her turn to take care of him. He wasn't ready for a nursing home, and he didn't really require that level of care. He just needed a gentle reminder to take his pills every day. And to not climb ladders, carry heavy objects, leave the pot boiling on the stove or drive at night.

Jackson placed two water bottles in front of her. "Make sure you drink all of this. We need to stay hydrated."

She thanked God for the meal He had provided, downed as much of the water as she could and then dug into her fries. Many people would have trouble eating after an ordeal like the one she'd lived through, but not her. Stress eating helped calm her nerves. She unwrapped her cheeseburger and took a huge bite.

Jackson had almost finished his meal before he spoke again. "I'm sure you want this over with as soon as possible. We might be able to help Cole move things along faster if we can figure out what the shooter and the guy in the muscle car are after."

"That makes sense, but I don't know much."

"You might be surprised at what comes to mind. If this was a crime TV show, they'd say to start with a motive. If you had to guess what the shooter was after, where would you start?"

She blew out a breath. "I suppose the first guess for anyone holding up a doctor's office would be that they wanted drugs, but he never asked for any."

"So, not an addict. What about a disgruntled client?"

"Disgruntled clients don't shoot their surgeon. They yell, threaten to sue and tell everyone who will listen how unhappy they are." She took another sip of water before reaching for the cheeseburger again.

"And it wouldn't explain why he shot Amy." Jackson gave her a moment to react to the mention of her friend's name.

"You're right." Her heart grew heavy, and she drew in a calming breath.

"Did Dr. Daniels do or say anything out of the ordinary recently?"

"He just went through a divorce." Bailey picked up a fry while thinking. "Maybe his ex-wife sent the killer."

"Why?"

"The divorce was her idea," Bailey said. "She must

have been angry with him for some reason. Maybe she was convinced he fooled around on her or that he was hiding money from her."

"Interesting." Jackson took a swig of water. "Do you think either of those are likely? If he was having an affair, maybe the shooter was his mistress's husband, looking for some revenge."

"Doctor Daniels wasn't the type to cheat—or to hide money. He was a good man, an honorable man."

"Well, if she wasn't angry with him for going behind her back—with money or with other women—then what reason would she have to hurt him?" Jackson asked.

Bailey's eyes went wide as an idea occurred to her. "Leslie is the beneficiary of an insurance policy."

"How do you know this?"

"I'm the bookkeeper. I make the payments. Plus, the doctor had me read over the yearly updates and summarize them during our informal meetings."

"Wouldn't he have made someone else beneficiary when they divorced?"

"He couldn't. It's not his policy. Leslie invested five thousand dollars of her own money in his practice during the early years. She's a co-owner of the business, so she took out a keyman life insurance policy, payable upon his death or inability to practice medicine due to illness or accident. Dr. Daniels said companies do this sort of thing." Bailey remembered the day he had griped about the premium payments. "He also said the policy was worth millions. I think someone should follow his ex-wife."

While drinking his water, Jackson considered the possibility that Leslie Daniels might have had her husband killed. Maybe the day's shooting wasn't connected to Dante Hill or his crime ring at all. Maybe he had tunnel vision here, assuming everything was connected to the case. He shouldn't ignore other possibilities.

He glanced in her direction and realized she was waiting for him to respond. He stopped and took a moment to really think it over…but then he shook his head. "It wouldn't be very smart for Leslie Daniels to knock off her ex-husband, especially if she's doing it for the money. The Slayer Rule means that if she's proven to have any connection to his murder, she loses all rights to any inheritance—including an insurance payout. Arizona's actually got the strictest laws in the country on the matter. If you ask me, she'd have been better off with him alive and alimony payments coming in."

Bailey frowned. "I guess that's true. And she *was* supposed to get a lot from him in alimony. But if not her, then who? I just can't imagine what reason anyone would have to kill him."

"Did Daniels do much traveling? Maybe he met someone who held a grudge against him," Jackson suggested. If Daniels actually was connected to the crime ring, maybe the surgeon had helped smuggle drugs.

"Depends on what you mean by 'traveling.'" Bailey reached for a french fry. "He bought an RV for his fishing trips. Leslie always stayed behind. She doesn't like roughing it. But they did take a California-beach vacation together every July."

"Hmm." Fishing trips could be a cover for illegal activity—or they could just be fishing trips. He just didn't know enough about the man to be able to say.

He walked over to the living room window and peered out through the blinds. A mother and daughter, leaving the pool area, gathered their towels and exited through the gate. Jackson noticed that the little girl's towel had a Euro Disney logo printed on it. "Do you know if your boss ever had any dealings with people from foreign countries?" Jackson asked on the way back to his chair. "Perhaps conferences outside the States?"

"The doctor is…" Sorrow altered her expression. "*Was*…a finicky eater. He had his favorite restaurants right here in the city and stuck to them. He had no desire to try anything new in a foreign country. He only went to medical conferences when he absolutely had to, and he'd never choose to go to one overseas."

She leaned back in her chair, looking thoughtful. "In the mystery movies I watch, the bad guy is usually the new person in town."

"Let's go with that," Jackson said. "Anyone come to mind?"

Bailey rubbed her forehead as if trying to force her brain to picture a stranger who looked out of place. Frustrated, she shook her head. "No. And why would someone from out of town want to hurt Dr. Daniels, anyway? I don't know why I brought it up."

"We're brainstorming. That's a good thing. One of your thoughts might lead Cole to the shooter, and then you can go home."

She blew an exasperated breath. "The sooner, the better."

"Let's try a twist on your idea. Did Dr. Daniels have any new or frequent visitors?"

"Other than pharmaceutical reps? Not really."

"Tell me about the reps."

"Stephanie knew most of them by name, and if anyone new showed up, she'd have the receptionist check their credentials before sending them back to the doctor's office."

"Stephanie—she was the practice's nurse, right?"

"That's right. She'd been with Dr. Daniels for years, and her desk was right by the reception area, so if she heard one of the reps out there, she'd come out to say hi."

"Did I hear that she moved?" Jackson asked.

"That's right—just last week. She came in one day and said that her husband had gotten a great job in Hawaii, starting right away." Bailey frowned, and Jackson was quick to notice.

"Something wrong?" he asked.

"It's nothing," she said, shaking her head, but her expression stayed troubled. Jackson just waited, letting her take her time figuring out what she wanted to say. "It's just…well, it seemed awfully fast. She didn't give any kind of notice—just said that she was leaving, and less than a week later, she was gone. I know her husband needed to be there right away, but surely she could have stayed a bit longer and headed to Hawaii later, don't you think? Dr. Daniels had to scramble to find a substitute for the surgeries he had scheduled. It just didn't seem like her to do that—not after working with him for so long."

Jackson's eyebrows shot up. The situation was sounding stranger and stranger by the minute. What had happened at the surgeon's office? What had the doctor gotten himself—and possibly his nurse—mixed up in?

Before Jackson could think of anything to say in reply, he heard several cars enter the complex, and the hairs on his neck stood on end. He lifted a finger to pause their conversation, then grabbed his Glock from the chair and headed to the living room.

Slowly, Jackson separated a window blind just enough to peer outside. He counted six armed men weaving between cars toward the various apartment buildings. "Hide in the hall," he whispered.

There went the last of his doubts that the doctor might have been killed for reasons that weren't connected to organized crime. No angry ex-wife or disgruntled former patient would have this many henchmen on call. But if all of this was being done on Hill's orders, then what was the man's endgame? Why was he devoting all of these resources to eliminate a witness who *might* be able to recognize a voice and provide a basic body description? What made Bailey so important?

Jackson flipped off the lights and pushed a padded chair against the door to buy them time if anyone tried to break in. The fact no one had headed straight to his apartment meant they didn't have his exact address.

Outside, a woman screamed, and a door slammed. Jackson stood beside the window to monitor the situation. Curious neighbors stepped outside, spotted the gunmen and then quickly retreated into their apartments, where they would hopefully call 911.

"How did they find us?" Bailey whispered from the corner of the hallway.

Jackson flinched. "I told you to hide."

"I need to know what's going on."

He rushed to escort her back down the hall, away from the living room. "There's a half dozen men out there hunting us down." By placing both hands on the wall, he trapped her with his stance and intense stare. "What do they want from you?"

She lifted her chin. "I told you, I don't know. I'm a bookkeeper, not a criminal."

He didn't think she was lying to him—not deliberately, anyway. But maybe there was something she knew that she hadn't yet realized was important. Only time would tell. He pushed away from the wall and huffed a breath. "We can't stay here, but we can't leave until the coast is clear, either."

She rubbed her hands over her arms. "That makes us sitting ducks."

FOUR

Bailey sat on the cold hallway tile, waiting for what seemed like hours. Finally, sirens wailed in the distance. Heavy footsteps pounded over concrete. Car doors slammed shut, and tires squealed. The bad guys were fleeing, and her heart sank faster than a heavy anchor. She had hoped for a police-force roundup.

Minutes later, squad cars swarmed the parking lot. Jackson strode through the living room to the window.

Bailey joined him, careful to remain hidden. "Do you recognize any of the officers? Maybe one we can trust to take us to a safer location?"

"Cole's not out there, and we can't risk trusting anyone else." He stepped away and gestured for her to follow.

She dropped onto the drab couch and held her head in her hands. Could their situation get any worse?

The sounds of neighbors gathering outside to check out the action carried through the closed window. Jackson didn't seem to notice. He filled a backpack with water bottles and trail mix, then looked through the blinds for what seemed like an eternity.

"Everyone left." He disappeared into a back room and returned shortly, wearing a long-sleeved dark blue shirt over a matching T-shirt while he stuffed some more clothes into the bag with the food.

When he bent to hand her a laptop, she noticed a bulge behind his right hip and suspected he now carried his gun in a waistband holster.

He shrugged on the backpack. "We have to get out of here. Now. My car is parked out front."

Her mind spun with possibilities. "Could they have hacked into the Department of Motor Vehicles to find us? If so, they know your car's make, model and license plate."

"It isn't registered in my name."

"Your home and vehicle are both in someone else's name?"

"I don't have time to explain. We need to go."

No. This did not feel right. She wanted answers, especially since she was putting her life in his hands.

Determined to stand her ground, she crossed her arms over her chest. "I'm not going anywhere with you until you give me an explanation. Maybe you've got your own reasons for living off the grid, but I don't think it's just chance that you landed right in the middle of…of whatever this is. What's your connection to all of it? Why does your brother let you take the lead even though he's the detective? What's going on here?"

"Bailey, we need to leave."

She tapped her foot, refusing to budge.

"All right, you win." With a stiff back and set jaw, he met her gaze. "When I started my job as the maintenance guy, I noticed that the dentist next door to Dr. Daniels was getting some suspicious-looking clients, and I told Cole about them. He staked out the parking lot and recognized a few from prior arrests on drug charges. We unofficially teamed up without the lieutenant's permission. I'm his eyes and ears at the medical center. I wasn't expecting what happened today, and I certainly didn't think that you, or Amy, or Dr. Daniels would end up in the line of fire, but I knew the situation was about to hit a tipping point. Cole and I have been on alert, waiting for it. That's all we have time for. Can we leave now?"

Every word rang true, although he as much as admitted it wasn't the whole story. Bailey dropped the subject. Temporarily. "Okay, let's go."

Jackson lifted his finger to his lips before unlocking his door.

The dead bolt clicked, and she shifted behind him. Worried someone could be standing nearby waiting for them, she hid behind his back. He tugged open the door just far enough to confirm they were alone and could exit the apartment. With each step, he scanned their surroundings and motioned for her to follow.

The concrete floor of the second-story walkway made it difficult to silence her footsteps. Somehow, Jackson didn't share her problem. Even wearing cowboy boots, he had a stealth-like walk, which only added to the mystery of the man.

She cringed at every sound she made on the steps. To his credit, Jackson never said a word or sent her a disapproving look.

Upon reaching the first floor, he checked to make sure no one lurked nearby before heading into the parking lot. She rushed to keep up.

He led her between two pickup trucks, crouching to stay out of view. She almost thought that they might make it to the car without any trouble…but then a bald man jumped up from behind one of the vehicles and slammed his fist into Jackson's face. He staggered back from the blow, then found his balance and dropped the backpack onto the asphalt.

Shocked, Bailey scurried to the front of the truck and hunkered down, leaning out just far enough to watch the two men battle. The muscular bald man blocked Jackson's right fist but couldn't avoid a punch to the gut when he followed up with his left hand. He doubled over while Jackson continued to fight back. Bailey's gaze fell onto the backpack.

She placed the laptop on the hood of the truck, ran to grab the backpack and waited for the right moment. The bald guy, who was too short to be the masked shooter, reached for the gun he had holstered at his hip.

With all the strength she could muster, Bailey swung the backpack, aiming for the gun held high in his hand. She misjudged her swing and struck the side of his head by mistake. Jackson followed up with a punch to the nose. The bald guy dropped his weapon, and his eyes rolled backward as he fell to the asphalt. She gasped. "Is he dead?"

Jackson, breathing heavily, confiscated the gun and patted down their assailant, then felt for a pulse. "Unconscious. He should be out for fifteen to thirty minutes."

"I've seen him before." She studied the attacker's round face and protruding ears—details she had learned to notice, working for a plastic surgeon. "He approached Dr. Daniels after work one day. They spoke in front of the office for about ten minutes." She glanced up at Jackson. "And no, I don't know what they talked about, and that was the only time I saw him."

"When did this take place?" Jackson dabbed at a spot of blood at the corner of his lip as he scanned their surroundings. Then he bent down to remove the bald guy's earpiece and two-way radio connected with a black wire.

"Over a month ago." With her heart racing, Bailey pointed to the device. "Can they hear us?"

"Not unless I push the button on the microphone."

"What are they? Mercenaries?"

He raised his brows in apparent surprise at her choice of words. "Less skilled. If they were mercs, we'd be dead. This guy wanted to land a punch before shooting."

"His mistake." She retrieved the laptop from the hood of the truck.

Jackson snatched his backpack by the strap, removed his keys from his pocket and pointed the fob at a black sedan parked a couple of rows away, directly in front of them. The headlights flashed.

Her eyes widened. "He was waiting for us here because they knew that car belongs to you. They know what we're driving."

"More likely, he watched us walk over here," Jackson answered. After snapping a picture of the unconscious man with the burner phone he'd retrieved from the trunk of his car, he sent it, along with a text, to his temporary DEA supervisor out of Phoenix. Need medic. My apt parking lot. Will call soon.

Bailey appeared to consider his answer. "Did you send the pic to your brother? Cole might have arrested him before."

"You're right. He might have." If Cole couldn't identify his attacker, another federal agent working the case might. The shooter and his accomplices could be guns for hire, or they could be members of the ring who had evaded arrest in Phoenix.

Jackson wiped off the communication device with his shirt and inserted it into his ear. He couldn't hear anything, so he made sure it was on. It was but the battery icon kept flashing, indicating a low charge. Bailey's expression reflected confusion. "I have to know what they're saying," he explained. "If we hear their next move, Cole might be able to catch them."

"Maybe you'll find out why they want me dead."

"I hope so." They climbed inside the sedan, and his gaze met hers. He wished he could make this all go away for her. "I'm glad to see you're feeling better."

"How can you tell?"

"You've been arguing with me." He turned over the engine and shifted into reverse.

"I wouldn't call it *arguing*." Bailey glanced down at the camera view on the dashboard. "He's gone!" She leaned over the center console and tossed the laptop onto the back seat. "Let's get out of here before he brings his friends back."

Jackson accelerated in reverse, careful not to hit the car parked behind him. Their jerky motions caught Bailey off guard, and she fell against his shoulder. He shifted into Drive with one hand while trying to steady her with the other.

"Sorry." She secured her seat belt while peering into her side mirror. "I thought he wasn't supposed to wake up for at least fifteen minutes."

"I was wrong. I'm doing the best I can in a tough situation." Jackson sped out of the apartment complex and zigzagged through traffic.

No one spoke for a long breath.

"I didn't mean to sound ungrateful." Bailey nervously scanned their surroundings. "Do you think that guy is the only one who stayed behind when the others left? I haven't seen anyone else who looks dangerous."

"Just because you haven't seen anyone else yet doesn't mean they aren't close by." The men searching for Bailey could be parked anywhere along their path.

"Where are we going?"

"Someplace safe where I can make a phone call."

"To Cole?"

"And a friend." He glanced over at her, knowing there would be questions if he didn't explain. "I want advice on what we should do next."

She nodded. "Makes sense. Neither of us is an expert on running from armed killers."

Inwardly, he cringed. Jackson hated not telling Bailey the whole truth, but he couldn't add to the danger she was in already. He'd made that mistake once and swore over the woman's dead body that it would never happen again.

Bailey pointed to a two-story brick building up ahead. "That's the new library. You can make your calls in the parking lot around back. I sincerely doubt a gunman would look for us there."

Arching a brow, he sent her an appreciative smile. She was proving to be a much better sidekick than he'd expected. With one more sweep of their surroundings, he parked in the back behind a dumpster. "Duck down. I'm going to keep my eyes on the road while I try to get in touch with Cole."

He stepped away from the car without waiting for a response. What he had to say, she couldn't hear. First, he texted Lily, his sister back at the ranch. New Phone. Give number to Cole in person, at home. He ended the message with his childhood nickname: Skinny.

Next, he leaned away from the smelly dumpster to study the main road in the distance while he called his supervisor in Phoenix. "Mike, you heard about the shooting in Sedona?"

"It's all over the news." The agent's no-nonsense demeanor came through loud and clear over the phone. "I've been waiting for your call."

"I have the surgeon's bookkeeper, Bailey Scott, with me." Jackson glanced back at the car, where she was still hidden from view. "She evaded the shooter, but we've been chased down by two different cars, and half a dozen gunmen invaded my apartment complex, searching for her. She says she doesn't know what they want. It could be as simple as eliminating a witness to the killings, but my gut says their motive is stronger than that. They're taking big risks, especially since she never even saw the shooter's face."

"You think the surgeon is connected to the dentist and the traffickers?"

"I do. No one else would have the resources to mount a manhunt like this for her." Jackson rechecked the road. No trouble in sight. "And she recognized the guy in the picture I sent you. She saw him speaking with Dr. Daniels over a month ago. By the way, you can call off the medical help. The guy who tried to kill me woke up and fled the scene."

"I'll make the call. Also, when I received your text, I pulled Martinez and Steele off their case. They're on their way up there. They'll search the surgeon's office if I can obtain a warrant. That's a big *if.* In the meantime, find a motel outside of Sedona to hole up in and text me your location."

"What about the bookkeeper? Shouldn't Martinez and Steele take her back to Phoenix, where she'll be safe?"

"Does she have evidence against the drug traffickers?"

"Not to my knowledge. Although she recognized the guy who attacked me in the parking lot, she can only tie him to the surgeon. No one else." Jackson knew where this was going, but he wanted better for Bailey.

"Then keeping her safe is up to the local authorities. Even with the leak, Cole can deal with this situation. It's not a federal matter. Unless…"

"Unless what?"

"The bookkeeper might know more than she realizes. Stick with her, talk to her and follow any leads that come up. If you can definitively tie the surgeon's death back to the drug traffickers, I might be able to offer her protection."

Not what Jackson wanted to hear. The danger from the shooter and his thugs seemed to increase with every confrontation. Jackson would do whatever he could to protect Bailey, but he was just one guy, up against at least a dozen. On the other hand, the danger wouldn't end until the criminals were caught, and if Bailey did know more than she realized, staying with her would give him time to find the answers to leave her truly safe in the end.

"Walker." The supervisor paused before saying, "She's safe with you. Do your job."

Jackson knew an order when he heard one. "Henderson is small and out of the way. I'll see if I can rent us a couple of rooms there."

After disconnecting the call, he headed back to the car. He didn't like the idea of continuing his charade with Bailey. He had grown tired of the lies and half-truths associated with undercover work. But he did have a job to do, and telling her the truth about it would only put her in more danger.

Bailey studied him as he eased behind the wheel. "What did they say?"

"I'm waiting for Cole to get back to me. I was able to reach my friend, though, and he agrees we should find a motel, but not here. I'm guessing the shooter will have men watching the three main roads out of town. We'll take the shortcut to Henderson."

"Isn't that an RV community?" Bailey asked as she settled back into her seat.

"It is." Back on the road, Jackson continued searching their surroundings for any sign of the armed men who had swept through his apartment complex. A red convertible pulled up next to them with two women wearing Sedona T-shirts. Tourists. "I knew someone who used to rent a room in Henderson when he visited his cousin. There are several motor home parks, a gas station, pizza parlor, convenience store and motel. Everything we need to stay under the radar."

"It is definitely the last place I would look for anyone." Bailey turned in her seat, studying the grocery store parking lot. There must not have been any suspicious characters, because she lost interest and turned back to watch the traffic again. "I've lived here for ten years, and I think I've heard the place mentioned once. Not in glowing terms. I don't remember a shortcut."

"Hardly anyone uses it."

She rolled her eyes. "Another dirt road? Did you drive quads over it when you were in high school?"

"Yes, it's a dirt road. No, I didn't drive my quad over it. Or my motorcycle." He felt her gaze fall on him and turned to exchange a quick smile. "Thanks for helping out with the bald guy."

A wave of pink washed over her cheeks. "It was the least I could do. You did save my life."

"You saved yourself first." Uncomfortable with the way his heart softened when he looked at her, he focused on the road up ahead. Jackson switched lanes and accelerated to drive around a slow-moving truck.

Bailey straightened in her seat, nervously jerking her attention from one vehicle to another.

"We're okay," he said, feeling bad for scaring her. "We're not being chased. I just didn't want us getting boxed in behind the truck."

She nodded. "Understandable." Seconds ticked by before she spoke again. "I got the impression you and Cole work well together. I'm surprised you didn't go into law enforcement, too."

While trying to think up an honest yet evasive answer, Jackson heard voices over the stolen communication device. He lifted his finger and pointed to his ear.

"Shadow Five, check in." The speaker, a man with a deep voice, sounded concerned.

Shadow Five? Maybe they were dealing with mercenaries after all. Either that or a group of drug traffickers who liked to think they were mercenary types.

Jackson rolled to a stop at a red light and cupped his hand around his ear, trying to block out the distracting traffic noise.

Another voice answered, this one sounding amused, "Shadow Five was taken down by the female target. His head is a bloody mess, and he isn't making much sense but says both were traveling on foot."

The bald guy must not have spotted them in the back of the parking lot. At least that answered the question as to whether or not the bad guys knew about his car.

"Shadow Two, where is the brother's car?"

Brother? Jackson's ire boiled in his gut. *Whose brother? They had better not be talking about mine.*

Another voice answered, "The cop's parked on Second Street. Two blocks away from the surgeon's office."

"Go see if he's trying to hide them again," the deep voice ordered.

Jackson tightened his grip on the steering wheel until his knuckles turned white. They *were* talking about Cole. "They have a tracker on my brother's car."

"No!" Bailey gaped at him.

"Shadow Five's radio is missing," came the second voice, this time not sounding so amused.

Silence followed. Jackson removed the device from his ear, switched off the two-way radio and stashed it inside the center console.

"What are you doing?" Bailey sounded bewildered.

"They know we're listening." When the traffic signal turned green, Jackson shot across the intersection. "And they've sent someone after Cole."

FIVE

Bailey tensed, watching cars and businesses whip by as Jackson raced down the street. What would the masked man or his accomplices do when they caught up with Cole? Or would the assailants find them first?

Why are they going to such lengths to find me, a book-keeper? Bailey wondered. Was the shooter so afraid she'd recognize his voice he was prepared to risk the lives of the men working with him in a gunfight with police? She found that hard to believe.

She stood on death's welcome mat and wanted to know how she'd landed there.

Jackson sped around a corner, and she gripped the door handle to keep from hitting her head against the window. After centering the car in the new lane, he pressed his thumb to his phone screen and passed it over to her. "Send a text to Cole. The—"

"You have the number for his burner phone?" she asked, cutting Jackson off.

"Not yet."

"I thought it wasn't safe to call his regular cell phone."

"It is for this. Trust me. Please. I have a plan." He rattled off Cole's number.

With lips pressed together, she suppressed her reservations and opened the messaging app. "What do you want to say?"

"Johnson Plumbing is en route to your location."

"Really?" She stared at him, dumbfounded. *What's wrong with "hightail it out of there before trouble arrives"?*

"Really," he stated in a no-nonsense tone.

"Okay." After sending the text, she glanced in Jackson's direction. His expression stern, he checked the time on his wristwatch. He hadn't even appeared this upset when the bald man hit him in the face.

"I'm sorry I was short with you," he said in a softer tone. "I had to warn my brother as fast as possible. I'm still afraid he might not read my message before trouble arrives."

"I understand," she said. Bailey didn't have a brother, but she did have her father, and she cared about him deeply. *Lord, please protect our loved ones and help us to return home safely. Soon.*

"If Cole calls, put him on speaker," Jackson instructed, interrupting her prayer.

"But we texted his hacked phone."

"He'll know the plumber message was from me and will call back with the burner. To be on the safe side, we'll ditch this burner and use my spare after I speak to Cole."

She wanted to question him as to why he had so many burner phones, but she knew that if she asked, he'd just give her a vague answer or no answer at all. This man had so many secrets. It should have made her wary of him—and it *did*. But in spite of that, she felt so safe with him. Safer than she'd ever felt with anyone before.

It suddenly dawned on her that once the bad guys were locked behind bars, she might not see the cowboy ever again. A sense of loss settled over her.

Why was she feeling this way? Could they have formed some sort of survivor's bond? Bailey studied his determined features beneath the Stetson and tried to make sense of him, but she felt like she wasn't getting anywhere. There was just too much she didn't know.

The phone rang, halting her string of random thoughts.

"Speaker," Jackson reminded her.

She pressed the correct button, and the detective's voice blasted through the phone. "Where are you? I just heard there were armed men near your place."

Apparently, the plumber message had worked as expected.

"Later. They're tracking your car and heading your way." Jackson raced down an empty side street. "One guy, maybe more. I counted six earlier. I'm on my way."

"No need," Cole replied in a rushed voice. "I have plenty of backup. We're checking out a lead on the shooter. Hide the package."

The package? Am I supposed to be the package? The call ended, and Bailey stared at the phone in her hands. "You have to tell me how Cole understood that crazy text."

Jackson exhaled a slow, steadying breath, then shifted to face her. A slight smile replaced his agitated expression. "Cole and I started sending each other coded messages in high school. It turned into a game. The odds were good he'd call to see if I sent this one."

"You two are so close. Makes me wish I had a sister." She rested her back against the seat. "What now?"

"Henderson." They made good time using the shortcut. Traveling the long way around would have taken them over forty minutes.

After reaching the only paved street in the area, they drove past a convenience store and a mobile home park with an old stagecoach marking the entrance. They finally rolled to a stop in front of a rundown motel.

Her gaze raked over the mostly empty parking lot and closed blinds in every window. "I don't think they're open for business."

"They are. The vacancy sign burned out years ago," Jackson said, shutting down the car's engine. "No one will look for us here, and no one renting a room will give us a second look or a second thought. The last time I was here, they didn't require a credit card, and the manager spends most of her time watching television in a back room."

Bailey took in the peeling paint on the walls and the wood rot surrounding the doors. "I'm surprised it hasn't been condemned."

"It looks better on the inside." He unbuckled his seat belt and grabbed his backpack. "Stay out of sight. The manager might get curious and look through the window after I check in. If these goons call motels to try to track us down, they'll probably ask about a couple."

"You might want to take off the hat. They'll probably ask about a cowboy, too."

"Good point." He placed his Stetson on the console between them.

"I'll be able to see the car through the office window. No one will sneak up on you." He left her alone with her thoughts.

Bailey felt foolish slipping down onto the floorboard

but did as he asked. He had managed to keep her alive so far. She credited God for guiding him.

She glanced down at the cell phone in her grip. Did she dare call her father? Jackson had told her not to earlier, but that was before he'd started using a burner phone. He had said that it was safe for Cole to call. And he planned to ditch this phone anyway. Why couldn't she call her father—just for a minute, just to let him know she was okay? If she waited until Jackson came back and asked for his permission, she had a feeling that he'd come up with another reason to say no.

Her father would be worried sick about her, and stress could compromise his health. That was all that mattered right now. She dialed the landline, hoping he was home to pick up.

"Hello?" The familiar voice sounded hesitant.

Hearing his voice broke Bailey's heart. She longed to go home right this second. She didn't know how much more of this she could take. "Dad, I can't stay on the phone for long. I just wanted you to know I'm all right."

"The police said there was a shooting in your office, and two people died." Fear punctuated every word he spoke. "Where are you?"

"I can only tell you that I'm okay. I'm with the handyman from the medical complex. His brother is a detective, and they are keeping me safe until the police catch the shooter."

"How long will that be?"

"I don't know. Soon, I hope. Call Uncle Steve and tell him to remind you to take your meds every night."

"Every night? You make it sound like this is going to go on for days."

How could she promise him otherwise when she

wasn't positive she'd ever return home? Her chest tightened and tears welled in her eyes.

"Dad, I have to go. I'm okay. Don't worry. I love you
very much." She ended their conversation, choked back
her emotions and deleted her father's number from the
phone's log of recent calls.

Bells chimed when Jackson stepped through the
motel-office door. The aroma of stale cigarettes attacked
his senses. A television blasted a home-improvement
show in the next room, which he found to be ironic.
From what he had seen, no one had lifted a finger to fix
up this place in years. While he waited at the desk, he
reached into his backpack to remove the phony driver's
license from his last undercover assignment and emergency cash he kept on hand.

"Good afternoon." The hotel manager appeared in
the open doorway. He remembered the petite thirtysomething brunette from the week Hawk's distant
cousin stayed here a couple of years ago.

"I'll be needing two connecting rooms. One for me
and one for my uncle. Around back, please." He hated
the way lying had become easy for him.

The manager reached the desk and checked him in
quickly, most likely eager to return to her show. Jackson
also purchased a travel kit for Bailey from the bookshelf
that served as a makeshift gift shop.

When he slid into the driver's side of his car, he whispered to Bailey, who was curled up on the floorboard,
"Stay down for another minute." He placed the travel
kit on the car's console, then drove around to the back
of the motel to their rooms, hidden away from anyone
on the main road. "The coast is clear."

Bailey climbed up onto the seat, looked around and grimaced. "I see this side doesn't look any better than the front." She rolled her eyes and sighed. "I'm sorry. I sound unappreciative."

"No need to apologize. Normally, I wouldn't recommend this place. But under the circumstances, it's our best choice. On the plus side, it doesn't look like they have many other guests tonight."

"I'm grateful for any place where I'm not likely to be shot. Thank you."

He gave a half nod, once again uncomfortable being thanked for doing his job. But then, she didn't know it was his job. She grabbed the laptop while he carried in everything else they might need.

"I asked for adjoining rooms." He escorted Bailey inside. "Yours is this way." He placed his belongings on top of the dresser, then unlocked and opened the door near the television. A quick search confirmed her room matched his and was safe for her to enter. A patchwork quilt covered a queen-size bed, and a small round water-stained table separated two white wooden chairs near the window. The furnishings appeared as old as the threadbare carpet, but they were clean.

He pulled the sun-faded drapes closed over the window blinds for extra protection from prying eyes. "This is your home away from home. I'll give you some time to freshen up, but then we need to talk."

She returned the half nod and closed the door.

After dismantling the burner phone, Jackson used the spare to text his supervisor and Cole, now that he had his brother's burner number. The police lieutenant had agreed it would be best if they kept Bailey's whereabouts confidential.

Jackson removed a water bottle from the backpack, then stretched out on the bed with the television remote in his hand. The local news zoomed in on the yellow caution tape surrounding Bailey's office at the medical complex, then cut away to helicopter footage of the two of them standing beside his SUV after the shooter ran them off the road and down the hill.

Raising the volume, he could hear, "According to reliable sources, two employees of the medical complex survived the shooting but later lost control of their car after being forced off the road."

The camera from the helicopter had focused on Bailey's face, making it even more difficult for them to hide now. If they didn't take precautions when on the move, someone was bound to spot her and call in their location to either the news station or the police department— which meant, thanks to the leak, that the shooter could learn their whereabouts wherever they went. At least Jackson's Stetson had obscured the top half of his face.

Rapping sounded on the connecting door.

"Come on in!" he hollered and rolled off the bed.

Bailey entered and immediately spotted the late-afternoon news rerunning their video coverage. Her jaw dropped. "Why aren't they showing the masked man?"

"They might not have had clear footage including him, or the lieutenant might have convinced them to wait." Jackson handed her a water bottle, then dragged his two chairs away from the window.

He waited for her to choose a seat before he joined her. "We need to help Cole catch these guys so that you can go home."

Bailey gripped her pendant, and he realized she did

so whenever they discussed going back home to her father.

Jackson reached over and squeezed her free hand. The simple move chiseled away a brick from his emotional wall. And even though he knew he should let go, he didn't. Instead, he gave them both time to process the horrible events of the day.

Jackson found himself remembering the times he'd spoken to Amy, the plastic surgeon's receptionist. She had been so young and full of energy. Any life wasted was a tragedy, but the young ones hit him the hardest, on the rare occasions when he allowed himself time to reflect and feel. The rest of the time, he had become good at compartmentalizing. But that was a gift that seemed to be failing him at the moment.

For some reason, it felt harder than he had expected to take his hand away from hers and focus on the case. A *lot* harder. He was only able to do so by reminding himself that solving the case would make her safer in the end.

Jackson waded into the conversation slowly, afraid she might stop helping him if she knew what he suspected about her former boss. "Remember the tattooed, gang-type guys I told you about?"

"The ones with great teeth, thanks to the dentist working next door to our office?"

"The ones with prior charges for drug dealing," he added.

"You said you were your brother's eyes and ears at the medical complex." Bailey tilted her head and met his gaze. "Did you see or hear anything you haven't told me about yet?"

He felt like he was on the witness stand. "Nothing

Cole could use, but I think they're running drugs through the dentist's office."

"And the office shooting is somehow related," she concluded. "But how can that be? If you think Dr. Daniels was in cahoots with drug dealers, you're wrong."

He held up his hands in a gesture of surrender. "I didn't say that."

"But you think it might be true." She narrowed her eyes at him. "The fact you haven't denied it proves my point."

"I'm considering all possibilities," he tried to explain matter-of-factly. "That is what Cole does."

"Well, I'm *not* considering that possibility." Bailey pressed her lips into a thin line. "But Cole will, won't he?"

Jackson nodded.

"Then I need to do something to convince him of Dr. Daniels's innocence." She rubbed her hands over the sudden goose bumps traveling down her arms. Seconds ticked by before she spoke again. "If something illegal really is happening at the dentist's office, Dr. Daniels might have seen or heard something and threatened to take it to the police. It could explain why the shooter went into his office with him, if he thought that the doctor had pictures or video either recorded on his phone or saved on his computer."

"That's a good point," Jackson agreed. It did make sense—and it fit with what he'd observed, including the conversation between the dentist and the surgeon. His gut told him that there was more going on—something that would explain why the thugs were chasing after Bailey so hard, but he couldn't discount this possibility.

"If the shooter wanted to search the doctor's house,

wouldn't he have sent one of his henchmen to do it immediately before or after the shooting?"

Jackson eyed her speculatively. "What are you thinking?"

"We should sneak into the doctor's house, take a look around, see what we can find. Dr. Daniels saved all his files to the cloud, but he had direct access on both his home and work computers."

"'We'? You're asking me to commit a crime."

"Yes, *we*. I'm the only one who will search for proof that Dr. Daniels was an innocent witness and not some kind of drug dealer. As for it being a crime, the doctor isn't in a position to file trespassing charges." Regret altered her expression.

Jackson did not want to take her to the house. "I'll tell Cole about the cloud account, and he can get a warrant."

"And the leak in the police department will warn the drug dealers."

Bailey made a valid point, but he wasn't ready to give in and take her.

Jackson grabbed his phone off the table to text his brother. Bailey thinks the doctor might have witnessed something at the dentist's office and saved evidence on his home computer. Can you search by yourself?

Cole answered in seconds. All computers at home and work have a virus. Techs going over them. Searches turned up nothing helpful.

"Well?" Bailey arched a brow.

"Did you know the computers all had a virus on them?"

Her expression turned grim. "I don't know about

mine, but Amy would have said something if hers had one. So would Dr. Daniels."

"Maybe the shooter wanted in his office to upload a virus to the network. He could have made sure they were all infected before the police showed up."

"The doctor would have had a backup," Bailey said, stubbornly insistent. "A printout, or a flash drive or something. He was careful like that. And if it's in his house, I think I could find it. We should sneak over there late tonight."

"We could have Cole—" Jackson said, but Bailey cut him off.

"Who is more likely to spot anything meaningful? Someone who worked for Dr. Daniels for over ten years or someone who never met him?"

She made a compelling argument. Plus, Jackson knew the shooter had already planted the virus and left the house, which meant it should be safe. And Jackson had been ordered to follow any leads Bailey could provide. Since there were enough dots to connect the surgeon to the bald guy who'd tried to kill him—a DEA agent—in the apartment parking lot, his group supervisor should be able to get a search warrant.

"I know the security codes to get in." Hope filled her eyes.

"And you're going to keep them a secret unless I bring you with me?" He forced back a smile. It was cute how she thought she had him in a bind when he'd already decided to take her along.

Bailey shrugged. "I'm the only one who wants to prove he's not in cahoots with drug dealers."

SIX

Bailey glanced out the window when Jackson drove up to the gate surrounding Dr. Daniels's community. "The keypad is finicky. You'll need to press each number slowly." She rattled off the plastic surgeon's birthday, ending with the pound sign.

Jackson entered the numbers and symbol, then looked at her long enough to make her uncomfortable, especially since she couldn't read his expression in the dim light.

She crossed her arms over her chest. "What?"

"How many times have you been here?"

"Once. Is that a problem?"

The iron gates parted, allowing them access to the homes of the rich and not-so-famous. Instead of answering her, Jackson pressed his foot down on the accelerator.

"The doctor's house is at the end of this road," she said, wondering why he cared how many times she'd been here.

They drove silently past silhouettes of trees and shrubs with only solar-powered ground lighting guiding them. Her stomach sank. This wasn't a friendly visit. They were here to learn why a ruthless killer had taken innocent lives.

When the adobe-style home came into view, she pointed to two wall lanterns lighting up the front entrance. "You can park in the next-door neighbor's driveway. They're gone for the summer. If a neighbor knows Dr. Daniels was killed, they might call the police if we park in front of his house."

Jackson turned where she directed and rolled toward a beige-colored garage door. "You say you've only been to the doctor's house once?"

She found his tone highly offensive. "Yes. Once. Nothing sordid was going on between us. Our relationship was strictly professional."

"Sorry. I didn't mean to give you the impression I thought otherwise." His apology sounded sincere.

Wishing he would tell her what he was thinking, she explained, "I know the neighbors are away because Dr. Daniels mentioned he was able to get a good night's sleep now that the owners are no longer swimming until two in the morning."

Jackson shut down the engine and pocketed his keys. "I had a neighbor like that once."

"What did you do?"

"Moved."

Short and to the point. No room for argument. She'd have to remember his technique the next time she wanted to end a conversation.

With the moon and stars shining brightly above them, they crept between the tall bushes dividing the two properties and entered the doctor's backyard through the unlocked gate. Jackson handed her a palm-sized green flashlight. "Wait until you get inside to turn it on."

Seconds later, she watched Jackson tug on the locked sliding glass door. When it wouldn't budge, he removed a pocketknife from his boot, then slid the blade between the frame and track. While pushing down to lift the glass, he reached up to yank on the handle. The door opened with ease.

Shocked by how easy it was to break in, Bailey made a mental note to add bars and extra locks to her back door.

At some point, the alarm had been deactivated, allowing Jackson to enter the doctor's house with Bailey following close behind. The beam from his phone's flashlight app first landed on an oak dining table and four chairs, then swung over the kitchen.

He abruptly stopped and stretched out his hand to keep her from entering the room. "The police wouldn't have made this mess. And Cole would have mentioned seeing it."

Every drawer had been tipped over and gutted. Cabinet doors stood open, the contents pulled down to litter the floor in messy heaps. She rubbed the pendant dangling from her necklace. Her only connection to her former life. "What were they searching for?"

"Whatever Daniels wouldn't give them." Jackson reached behind his back for the gun hidden in a waistband holster. He lifted his finger to his lips. "They might not have left," he whispered. "Turn off your light."

Bailey soon lost sight of him, and her pulse quickened. She listened to his footsteps traveling from room to room and tried to find comfort in the fact there were no other sounds, but seconds still felt like hours. She continued to rub her pendant.

The beam of a flashlight flickered on the walls near the kitchen. *Please be Jackson.*

What if it's not him? Her body tensed.

The shadow of a man wearing a cowboy hat turned the corner, and she breathed a sigh of relief. Jackson might not be a police officer, but his bravery made her feel safe—even though she had the feeling there was more to him than he cared to share.

"They've turned over every inch," Jackson said, "but we still might uncover a lead. Anything to tell us what's going on here." He slipped his gun back into the holster.

"Let's check his office."

"After you." He gestured toward the hall.

Bailey stood in place until she captured Jackson's full attention. "Just so you know, Daniels sent me here to pick up his cell phone when he forgot to bring it to work. That's how I know his gate code and which room he uses as an office. In case you were wondering."

"I'm not."

"Good." Dropping the issue again, she stepped forward. Her memory replayed the day the doctor had sent her here for the phone. He *had* been preoccupied. She hadn't paid much attention because nothing had been normal since the day his marriage started falling apart. But now she couldn't help wondering. Were there other things that had been weighing on his mind? Things he'd seen? Things he'd…done? She didn't want to believe it—but then, she hadn't wanted to believe that her fiancé was lying to her, either.

Bailey shined the beam of the flashlight into a bedroom, and her breath caught in her throat. Someone had ripped up the mattress and pillows. The remains littered the area rug like confetti. These people were determined to find what they wanted. No matter what or who got in their way.

Jackson placed a hand on her shoulder. She relaxed beneath the warm strength of his touch and continued her trek down the hall.

The condition of the office was slightly better than the other rooms but only because there were fewer items to gut and shred. Jackson stepped over the office supplies strewn across the tile floor and sat behind the doctor's empty desktop. The police had taken the computer and its various parts.

While Jackson tugged open drawers, she scanned the room with her flashlight beam. There was no file cabinet or box filled with paperwork. Her gaze eventually fell onto a thin object wedged between the desk and the wall. It must have fallen there before or during the search. "Can you reach that?"

He picked up a plastic ruler from the floor and used it to sweep the space until he retrieved what turned out to be a pamphlet for a marina near Phoenix with a receipt stapled to the back. "Did you know the doctor owned a boat? He paid in advance to keep it stored at Lake Pleasant for a year."

Bailey frowned. "No. He never mentioned it."

"Interesting." Jackson sounded like a prosecuting attorney.

She jumped to her employer's defense. "Not bragging about a boat doesn't mean he bought it with drug money. My two uncles, a cousin and my former fiancé all own boats." She felt her face tighten at the mention of the man who had been the worst mistake of her life. Not wanting Jackson to notice her expression, she turned away to sort through the office supplies on the floor.

Jackson let it drop and rummaged through the closet. The pockets of the doctor's winter clothing had been pulled out before being tossed into a pile on the floor. "They're looking for something small. Maybe a key or thumb drive."

Bailey shined her light on the empty shelving unit. The books that had once been neatly arranged were now scattered in a corner, along with a wall calendar. The need to snoop through the pages grew more urgent, and she hurried over.

The calendar was open to the current month. The fact that there were no notations for July explained why the police hadn't thought to take it with them. In June, the doctor had scribbled a note to send his sister a birthday card. Bailey bit her lip to keep from crying. The stay-at-home mother lived in Philadelphia with her husband and four kids. And today she would be notified of her brother's death.

Bailey forced back her tears. While viewing the page for May, words printed in small letters stood out like a billboard. "Early consult."

"What?" Jackson glanced in her direction.

"He noted an early Saturday consult on his calendar." She showed him the page as her mind raced to recollect the events of that morning. "I remember it. I showed up early that day to catch up on billing I had missed while out sick. The patient was a woman who knocked at the front door an hour before we were scheduled to open."

"For it to have made such a strong impression on you, I'm guessing that this was no ordinary appointment."

"You're right. I was about to unlock the door and speak to her when Dr. Daniels cut me off in the lobby. He said he would handle it, that she was his friend's daughter, and he planned to talk her out of having rhinoplasty. I went back to work. When they walked by my office, I couldn't get a better look at her nose because she was facing the opposite wall."

"Did she have the surgery?"

"I don't know. I don't remember seeing her again, but then the exam room isn't near my office. Unless I happen to cross paths with them coming in or going out, I usually only interact with a patient over the phone."

Jackson leaned against the desk and crossed his arms over his chest. "If Daniels made the appointment when he was at home, that would explain why he marked his wall calendar. The consult might not have anything to do with the shooting, but you have me thinking. Maybe he was attacked because of a surgery he performed. What were you telling me earlier about his nurse—that she left and he had to scramble to find someone to fill in? Did she assist in surgeries?"

"Yes, Stephanie assisted with all of them."

Jackson tilted the brim of his hat. "If Cole can bring you your phone, can you call Stephanie? She might know if something connected to one of the doctor's surgeries is why someone would want you all dead."

Bailey's heart dropped. "I didn't think anything of it at the time, but… I tried to call her yesterday, just to check in and see how she was doing, and…"

"And?"

"The number was disconnected." She met Jackson's gaze. "We need to find her."

Glad the DEA had obtained a search warrant for the house, Jackson continued rummaging through each room for any information that might shed more light on the case.

"Let's try the garage." Jackson led the way. Inside the garage, he aimed his cell phone flashlight on the wall lined with cabinets. They were closed, unlike the ones in the kitchen. Something about that felt strange. Why wouldn't the men who had trashed the rest of the house have searched the garage as well?

Bailey stepped behind him. The hint of her floral perfume wafted through the air, distracting him momentarily. "I'll look in here."

"I'll start at the other end." Bailey carried a step ladder into the center of the garage and positioned the small flashlight on top, shining the beam onto her work area.

Following her lead, he propped up his cell phone on top of the water heater so that the beam would help him conduct his search. At this angle, they were unlikely to attract the attention of any neighbors.

Jackson reached into the first cabinet and pulled back the lid to a plastic box filled with fishing gear. Why anyone would own over twenty different types of fishing line was beyond him. He dug around for hidden thumb drives, photos or paperwork that might divulge information pointing to the killer.

Bailey tugged open the tallest cabinet and gasped. A man leaped out, grabbing hold of her neck with both hands while pushing her up against the step ladder and knocking the flashlight onto the garage floor. She squirmed, kicked and scratched while gasping for air.

Jackson whipped his Glock from his holster and aimed it at the attacker's dimly lit head. "Let her go, or I'll shoot!" He narrowed his eyes into slits and gripped the weapon tighter. "Now!"

"Don't shoot." A young man, barely out of high school, reached for the ceiling. He stepped back away from Bailey, who grabbed on to the stool for support, gasping, coughing and rubbing her neck with her free hand.

Relieved she was all right, Jackson reached out for her. He kept his focus on the kid with a crooked nose and shaggy hair as she held on to Jackson's arm and leaned against his shoulder.

The kid didn't exude the same sinister persona as the other men back at the apartment complex. He looked more like a juvenile delinquent who stole cars and sold them to chop shops. He also wasn't carrying a two-way radio.

"Slowly turn around and place your hands behind your back." Jackson waited for him to comply before stepping closer to the box full of fishing line.

"There's duct tape on the kitchen floor." Bailey coughed on her words, snatched the flashlight off the concrete floor before disappearing into the next room.

"What's your name?" Jackson barked.

Silence.

"Who do you work for?"

The kid lifted his head defiantly in the air.

A quick pat-down revealed he didn't carry a phone or identification. Jackson pocketed the switchblade he found concealed in a sock. "What were you looking for when you made this mess?" Not a word. Not even a denial. "I asked you what you were looking for."

"Do I look stupid?" The hoodlum's harsh, arrogant tone filled the garage.

"Yes, you do." He was so tired of these guys jumping out at them. "You made two trips here to do something that could have been done in one."

"We didn't know the surgeon hid something until after we wrecked his computer," the kid scoffed. "And he might have lived long enough to tell us where he hid it if he hadn't fought for the gun."

Jackson could tell by the kid's build—and also by his general air of inexperience—that he wasn't the shooter, so he must have heard all of this from the other traffickers. "What did the surgeon hide?"

The kid shrugged.

Thoroughly annoyed, Jackson pressed on. "Why did you attack an innocent woman?"

"It's not my fault she knows too much."

"You were ordered to kill her, specifically? Why? Because she saw the shooter?"

"She *knows* too much," the smart-mouthed kid repeated. "Are you deaf?"

Was Bailey hiding something to protect herself? Or the doctor's reputation? It was hard to believe—but it got him back to the idea that she might know more than she realized. Jackson tilted back his hat and wiped away the beads of sweat clinging to his forehead. "What does she know that's worth killing over?"

"If I knew and I told you, I would die."

What a fool. "And you think they'll just take your word for it that you kept your mouth shut, even when I had a gun to your head? They'll assume you told me everything you knew to save your own skin, and then they'll find a way to kill you in prison. The goons you're hanging around with don't leave loose ends."

At that, the boy finally started to lose some of his confidence. "But if you actually do cooperate, I might be able to help you become a protected witness. Otherwise, you have a nice, long stretch of time in prison to look forward to when you're tried as an accomplice to today's murders—if you even make it that long."

"I didn't have anything to do with that shooting," he said between clenched teeth.

"You're an accomplice after the fact. Not to mention the attempted murder—here, just now."

"All right! The doctor hid a thumb drive. I don't know what's on it, only that there aren't any thumb drives here or on his boat. Now, get me off the murder wrap, and make sure I don't end up in the same prison yard as the rest of them."

"I'll see what I can do."

Bailey pushed open the door and dragged in a wooden dining room chair behind her, keeping her distance from her attacker. In her free hand, she held the flashlight and a pair of scissors. She also wore a roll of duct tape like a bracelet. When the beam of light flashed over her face, he could see her color had returned, and she appeared to be her usual self. He also spotted the red marks on her neck, which made him frown.

He took hold of the chair. "No sudden moves, kid. This Glock is two inches from your head."

"What are you going to do to me?" His voice cracked before finishing the question.

"Are you ready to explain what she knows?"

The kid frowned. "What, you think they actually told me?" Jackson stopped to consider it. It was possible the kid really didn't know. It was also possible he was bluffing. Either way, they didn't have the time to find out.

"Remember the gun." Jackson grabbed the kid's shoulder, pulled him down onto the chair and then reached behind his back toward Bailey, who handed him the tape. "No one is going to hurt you," he said.

The kid flinched.

Once Jackson had him secured to the chair, he texted his supervisor. Doctor's house. Guy tried to attack Bailey. Tied him up in garage. Remembering the two-way radios, he added, Need AAA batteries. The radio might come in handy, and he didn't want it dying on him.

The return text read, On it.

Jackson cut off a final strip of duct tape, stretched it over the kid's mouth and turned to Bailey. "You're resourceful."

She shrugged. "It helps when everything you need is piled on the floor, thanks to this guy."

"True." He placed his hand on her back to lead her out of the garage, and his cell phone suddenly rang. He recognized Cole's burner number on the screen when he answered. "Good news?"

"I wish." His brother hesitated. "The new local reporter is claiming that Bailey called her father to tell him you kidnapped her."

Jackson gaped. He resisted the urge to turn and look at her. He wanted to demand answers, but this was not the place to hold this conversation.

"The network stations won't touch the story because Bailey's father hasn't confirmed it, but it's all over the cable-news shows," Cole continued. "They're even showing a close-up picture of your ID badge. The one for the medical complex. They kept it up so long I could see the scar on your cheek."

"Tell me you're kidding." Jackson knew he wasn't, but he couldn't wrap his brain around why her father would say something like this. If he did.

"It gets worse," Cole warned. "The lieutenant believes the story. He thinks you went there today to kidnap her—that the doctor tried to stop you, and that is why you killed him and the receptionist. I've been trying to clear this up with Bailey's father, but he's not answering his phone or the door. But he did leave us a message about Bailey calling him—though the message didn't say she'd been kidnapped."

Jackson's gaze fell on Bailey. What on earth was going on? "Cole, I'll text you after I handle this new development."

SEVEN

Bailey fidgeted, feeling unsettled by Jackson's penetrating stare. "What happened now?"

"We'll talk later." He headed to the door, still carrying the duct tape.

Suddenly, Bailey felt all alone. Why was she so upset to have him withdraw from her? She didn't know this man. He had admitted to keeping his life private on purpose. And today had only proved she couldn't trust anyone besides her father. Even Dr. Daniels had kept a dangerous secret from her. She just hadn't figured out what it was.

Jackson led the way through the kitchen to the back door. He held it open and stared straight through her. Her stomach clenched. She had no idea why Jackson was upset with her. Could it be something she forgot to mention after the shooting? Did Cole discover information about her boss they assumed she knew?

Oh, no. She grasped the pendant dangling around her neck. This had to be about the phone call to her father. "I—"

"Save it." He took the lead back to the sedan, not seeming to care if she stayed close to him or not.

The second he toggled the car locks, she jumped inside and buckled her seat belt. Dragging in a deep breath, she searched for the right words. Jackson tossed the tape onto the back seat, turned over the engine and shifted into Reverse. Still not speaking to her. There was no need to when the look on his face spoke volumes.

A mile down the road, Bailey couldn't stand it any longer. "Yes, I called my father. And yes, I used your phone while you were in the motel office, getting our rooms—and then I deleted the call off the log so you wouldn't see it. I'm sorry. I needed to let him know I was okay. He has heart disease, and stress could cause a heart attack."

Jackson jerked the car to the curb and shifted in his seat to stare her down. "Did you tell your father I kidnapped you?"

"What?" She pulled back away from him in disbelief. "I *never* said that."

"That's not what a reporter is claiming. She's making sure every person in this state studies my picture to help 'save' you from me if they happen to see either one of us. And Cole's lieutenant thinks I shot Amy and Dr. Daniels when they tried to protect you from me."

"There has to be some sort of misunderstanding." Bailey struggled for an answer. "Or the reporter is making this up for ratings…" She threw her hands up in the air. "I don't know why she would say something like that, but she's *wrong*."

Just when Bailey thought nothing could get any worse, her only lifeline was turning on her. A thought occurred to her. "I know for a fact my father wouldn't speak to a reporter. He doesn't trust them. And now I understand why."

Jackson narrowed his eyes. "If he wouldn't have talked to a reporter, then how would she even know you called him?"

"Maybe the leak at the police station planted the story? Though I'm not sure how the leak would know I really did call my dad."

The hard lines in Jackson's jaw refused to soften, but he grew quiet as if considering the idea before finally admitting, "Your dad called the station and said that he'd heard from you. The leak could have heard that message." He checked for oncoming traffic, then drove away from the curb. At least he wasn't speeding like before. That was a good sign.

A multitude of thoughts collided in her mind. She stared out the window, unable to focus on anything they passed. She hated the thought that Jackson's reputation would take a hit just because he'd helped her. "You've risked your life to protect me," she said, glancing over at him. "I would never claim you kidnapped me."

At least five minutes passed before he finally spoke, his voice hard. "The leak could have made up the story, but the fact you used my phone and didn't tell me makes it difficult to trust you. Whether you meant to or not, your actions have made us less safe."

"But how?" That was the last thing she wanted. "You said burner phones were okay to use. Isn't that what your last phone was? A burner?"

"Yes, but you can't make random calls. The number could end up in the wrong hands, and they could trace it back to us. Besides which, the fact that this turned into a news story means that our pictures are all over the place. If someone spots us, they'll call it in to the police—and the leak will let our attackers know where to find us."

"I know, and I'm sorry," she said softly. "It never crossed my mind that this would happen. I just wanted to let my father know that I was okay. I had no idea this would be the end result."

Some of the tension eased out of Jackson's shoulders. "I believe you," he said, simple and quiet. Neither of them said anything for a stretch after that, but the silence didn't feel tense or awkward anymore.

Jackson pulled into a drive-through fast-food restaurant for a late dinner. She felt guilty allowing him to pay for her chicken-tender kids meal, but she didn't have much choice. "Do you think your brother can remove my purse from the crime scene soon? I need my wallet."

"If it's money you're worried about, don't. I can cover whatever it is you need. Cole will give you your purse when he can."

"Thank you. I'll pay you back."

His eyes softened, and he smiled for the first time since he had gotten so upset. "You can make me brownies again when this is all over."

Bailey wouldn't mind baking for him again, but she doubted he'd still be around. He'd told her this job was just temporary. Surely his next position would be starting soon. The thought brought on mixed feelings. She did care about the man, and she wished she could get to know him better. But that didn't seem to be an option.

On the drive back to the motel, Bailey reached inside her kids-meal bag and found a plastic doll with yellow hair. She placed it on the center console, then retrieved a straw, removed the wrapper and poked it through the lid of her soda cup.

After parking, Jackson ushered her into his room to eat their meal. She eased onto the uncomfortable wooden chair and placed her box of chicken tenders and soda cup on the small round table between them. He took her empty bag and tossed it into the trash before grabbing the package of AAA batteries sticking out of his backpack. An odd expression flickered across his face as he ripped apart the cardboard to remove the contents.

"What are those for?" she asked, selecting the largest chicken tender.

"The two-way radio." He pried open the back of the device he'd taken from the bald man who attacked him in the apartment parking lot and traded out the batteries.

"Aren't we out of range?"

"We are, but if those guys come looking for us, we might hear them. Advanced warning could help us escape."

She nodded. "But they know we have one of their radios. Why would they keep using them?"

"I'm hoping they stayed off long enough to think we'd given up on listening to it. I believe they'll try again on a different frequency if they're avoiding phones. Cellular companies keep records and can tie them together through calls and texts."

"It would be nice to have advanced warning." She continued eating, and he eventually joined her.

"I did learn something from the guy in the garage," he said, removing his burger from the bag. "They aren't after you because you saw the shooter."

Her eyes widened. "Then why are they targeting me?"

"Apparently, you know too much."

She held up a chicken tender. "But what would I know?"

"We need to figure that out if we want to help Cole."

She could only think of one thing to do. "I'll pray on it tonight." She rubbed her pendant, missing her old life while starkly aware everything had changed forever. Except God's love. It never wavered. She silently asked Him to shine a light on the unknown.

After eating and updating both Cole and his supervisor, Jackson shoved the remaining AAA batteries into his backpack. It had been a surprise to come back to the room and discover that a DEA agent had slipped inside while they were out and left behind a large-enough package of batteries to keep the two-way radio running for days. To his relief, Bailey hadn't asked any questions about them, although her expression clearly revealed she hadn't remembered seeing the batteries sticking out of his bag earlier.

Jackson's phone vibrated in his pocket, signaling a text message. Bad news from Agent Martinez. Green muscle car headed to Henderson.

"What is it?" Bailey watched him with worried eyes.

"We should prepare for unwanted company." He tucked the ends of his long-sleeved shirt into the back of his jeans, providing easy access to his waistband holster behind his right hip.

Her eyes grew wide. "Did they find us?"

"Hard to say. Someone's headed in this direction, but I can't be sure if they know our exact whereabouts or just have an idea that we headed out this way. Still, we shouldn't take any chances. If he *does* stop at the motel to see if we're here, there's a decent chance the manager would give him our room numbers. Let's get out of here."

They hurriedly packed up their sparse belongings, and Jackson led her along the back of the motel, passing by a half dozen doors and windows with closed blinds. The only sounds came from the heels of their shoes hitting the concrete path. He stopped at the corner of the building to wield a lock-picking kit he'd removed from his backpack.

Bailey held her travel kit to her chest with both hands while searching the shadows surrounding them.

He entered the dark room, guided by the light bulb hanging outside near the door. A musty aroma permeated the air, assuring him the room had been unoccupied for a while now.

"What about the car?" she asked, gesturing over her shoulder.

"We don't have time to move it. Don't worry. I still don't believe they know what we're driving." He dropped his belongings at the foot of the queen-size bed, then removed the flashlight from his backpack and flipped it on.

Bailey glanced outside again before closing the door while Jackson pulled the drapes closed over the window blinds.

"Is Cole coming?" she asked in a nervous whisper.

"He won't make it here in time," Jackson said, not telling her who sent the text.

"Should we go somewhere else in case the manager tells them we're staying here?" she suggested. "Maybe the pizza parlor? We could walk there from here."

"We're better off staying out of the public eye as

much as we can. The world thinks I kidnapped you, remember?"

Bailey worried her lip. "Should I call home and tell my father to speak to the lieutenant? He might not know who to trust after the reporter lied about what he said."

"No." Jackson's firm tone held no doubt. "The shooter may have hacked into your father's phone since you last spoke." He paused before continuing. "And we don't know if the lieutenant is the leak."

Her jaw dropped. The thought obviously hadn't occurred to her.

"You can leave your travel bag on top of the dresser." He glanced at the connecting-room door. "And stay where I can see you until I know we're safe."

With a curt nod, she did as he requested, then stood against the wall in the dark. The small flashlight was packed in her travel kit, but she hadn't asked to use it.

He carried a wooden chair over for her. "Remember to whisper."

After removing the two-way radio from his backpack, he flipped off his flashlight and stood next to the window. He pushed aside the edge of the curtain to peer out through a slit in the blinds. The bulb outside cast a faint glow in the room.

Bailey grew restless behind him, rubbing her hands over her arms. "Can I search different frequencies for their voices? You won't have to take your eyes off the parking lot if I work the radio."

He decided it wouldn't hurt to have her take control of the radio. "Keep the volume low." He handed it over.

For several minutes, all he heard were clicks, humming and Bailey's uneven breathing.

The roar of a souped-up engine announced the arrival of the muscle car.

Jackson's pulse spiked.

"Shh," he warned while snatching his Glock from his waistband holster. He removed the safety and stood guard.

Bailey's breathing grew shallow. She moved to the carpeted floor behind the bed where she couldn't be seen through the window, taking the radio with her.

The muscle car growled as it drove out of the shadows and into the light. Jackson's jaw tightened. He continued to watch through the small slit while gripping his weapon tightly, ready to defend Bailey.

The shooter's accomplice parked near the trunk of Jackson's sedan, the only other vehicle parked behind the motel. A short, wide man—most likely the one who had followed them after the shooting—emerged from the driver's door, weapon raised and ready. He scanned the motel room windows before advancing.

Jackson stood perfectly still, fearing the man's gaze would connect with his if he detected motion. The man, now wearing a black jacket, walked over to the sedan and shined his phone's flashlight inside. To Jackson's shock, he seemed to deflate, relaxing his stance. He studied his surroundings once more before lowering his weapon on the way back to his car.

Is this a trick?

A gruff voice emanated from the other side of the bed. "Panther to Cobra. Come in, Cobra."

"It's the radio," Bailey whispered, lifting her head just enough to look at him from her hiding spot. "I found the new frequency."

Jackson lifted his finger to his lips, reminding her

to keep quiet to avoid being heard by the guy outside. No one could hear them through the radio unless they pushed the microphone button.

"Cobra here. Report." The deep voice belonged to the man in charge who had spoken through the device back at the apartment complex. Now they were using animal names instead of shadow numbers, as if that were enough to fool anyone.

"They're not here," the accomplice answered. "Panther out."

Cobra didn't bother to respond.

The muscle car's engine popped and thundered before it sped away.

Jackson watched the vehicle leave, barely able to believe his eyes. "What just happened?" he asked, dazed. "What made him decide, after one glance inside my car, that it couldn't belong to me?"

Bailey pushed against the side of the bed to stand. "It had to be the kids toy."

"What?" Jackson turned to make sure he heard her correctly.

"I left the toy from my kids meal on top of the car console."

He shook his head in disbelief. "Saved by a plastic doll?"

She joined him at the window. "How long do you plan to stand watch?"

"An hour or two." Jackson peered outside again. "To be on the safe side."

"We might as well get comfortable." She took hold of both chairs and started dragging them closer to the window.

He rushed over to help, and when he reached for

them, his fingers brushed over hers. Their gazes connected in the faint glow provided by the bulb hanging outside the door.

She spoke first. "Thank you again for protecting me."

He flinched, remembering why his supervisor had allowed him to stay by her side. "Bailey..."

"Yes?"

"I care about what happens to you." He wanted to kick himself. He sounded like an awkward teenager.

Confusion flickered through her expression. "I care about what happens to you, too."

Cold air seeped through the glass, and goose bumps traveled down his arm. He finished positioning the chairs, then used the flashlight to find an extra blanket in the closet.

When he returned, she had taken a seat, and he wrapped the heavy wool around her shoulders. She smiled up at him; then together, they studied the parking lot for over two hours.

Bailey yawned and pointed to the adjoining door. "I assume my room is in there."

"It is," he said, crossing over to pick the lock for her. "Try to get a good night's sleep."

Uncertainty flickered over her face. "I'm exhausted, but I'm afraid to close my eyes. I don't know which is worse—worrying a real monster will break down the door or knowing the one in my dreams will haunt me if I manage to fall asleep."

He could relate. "We all have nightmares." He didn't want to share his. Taking a life, even in the name of the law, was never easy. He remembered her faith. "Maybe if you pray, God will help you find peace."

"You're right. I need to hand over my concerns to Him. I can do all things through Christ."

"Some of these old motels still have Bibles in the nightstand drawers. It's worth checking." After unlocking the door, he stepped aside.

"That would be nice." She grabbed her travel kit off the dresser, stepped into the other room and closed the door behind her.

He was growing fond of having Bailey around, which was a dangerous feeling to cultivate. She would be furious if she knew the only reason his supervisor was allowing him to protect her was to gather any information she could provide.

With a troubled mind, Jackson slid open the nightstand drawer and did indeed find a Bible. The last time he read God's word, his faith had been strong. Not so much these days. Not with women and men constantly committing heinous crimes against humanity. Both young and old suffered needlessly. Why didn't God step in to save them? Part of him wanted to dig deep into the passages and find the answer. But not tonight. He pushed the drawer closed, but he did offer up a prayer. "Lord, please help me keep Bailey safe."

He eased into one of the chairs near the window to keep an eye out for any unwelcome visitors.

Jackson stood and stretched several times over the next few hours, moving around to make sure he stayed awake and alert. No one came or went from the motel's parking lot, and a million thoughts passed through his mind. He winced every time he thought of the news story out there framing him as a kidnapper. What would his life be like if his superiors forced him to give up his undercover work because his face had made national

news? It would be an embarrassing end to his undercover career. On the other hand, though, would he really miss the work? It would certainly be nice not to
have to lie any longer.

There was a rumor floating around that the governor
was looking for someone to lead a drug task force in the
northern part of Arizona. A state supervisory position
would mean leaving the DEA, but he'd be able to move
back home permanently. Also, no more undercover as-
signments. Something to consider.

A dark sedan with its headlights turned off rolled
into the parking lot and pulled into one of the empty
spaces. Jackson's pulse raced as he gripped his weapon.
The driver's-side door opened, and the car's overhead
light illuminated Agent Martinez's menacing face and
long, dark hair before the agent reached up and flipped
off the switch.

Jackson opened the motel door and leaned out just
long enough for the man to see him and walk to the
room with long strides.

Dressed in faded jeans and a dark hoodie, Martinez
could pass for a hoodlum skulking around in the dark,
up to no good. "I'm here to keep watch," Martinez announced, "so you can get some sleep."

"How long?" Jackson locked the door between rooms
to keep Bailey from walking in and discovering a stranger.

"Five hours." The agent took position at the window.
"Oh, and I'm supposed to tell you that kid we picked up
in the surgeon's garage has a record. His fingerprints
say his name is Karl Griffin, and he was arrested last
year on drug charges in Nogales, Arizona, but released
on a technicality."

"And?" Jackson stretched out on the bed.

"We tied him to Dr. York, that dentist you were watching," Martinez added with a grin.

Jackson arched a brow. "'Tied' how?"

"The dentist's wife is his cousin, along with a couple of other guys in the trafficking ring."

Jackson sat up with a start. "Now that's what I call interesting." They may have landed a significant lead here. "I'll pay Dr. York a visit first thing in the morning."

EIGHT

The following morning, Bailey sat in the parked car with Jackson, eating cherry Danishes and sipping the coffee they had ordered from the coffee shop's drive-through window.

They were both in better moods after a few hours' sleep and a shower. Jackson had changed into the dark green T-shirt he'd stuffed into his backpack. She was stuck wearing her yellow blouse.

She inhaled the aroma of vanilla creamer while scanning the coffee shop's parking lot for the tenth time. "Are you sure Dr. York comes here every morning?"

"Positive." Jackson pointed toward a black BMW entering from a busy street. "I followed him after I teamed up with Cole."

"What should we ask him first?" Bailey said, eager to start the dentist's interrogation.

"'We'?" He shook his head. "You're staying here. We don't know what to expect from this guy. He might have a weapon on him."

She pursed her lips, wishing she could argue even while knowing he was right. But looking back at the times she'd greeted the dentist in passing, she found it hard to believe he could be a hard-core criminal.

Jackson took one last sip of his coffee before getting out of the car and weaving between the parked cars on his way to the BMW.

I can't sit here doing nothing. She tapped her hand on her knee, watching Dr. York pull up alongside the other dozen vehicles near the coffee shop.

She wasn't sure Jackson would share everything he learned in the next few minutes. In her heart, she knew Dr. Daniels wasn't involved with dealing drugs, but he did keep a secret from her. One big enough to drive Stephanie away and to get him killed. Bailey wanted to know the truth. She *deserved* to know the truth.

With quiet movements, she slipped out of the sedan, then crouched while slinking from one car to the other. The back end of a full-size white pickup truck near the two men provided the perfect place to hide and listen.

"What are you doing here?" The angry voice belonged to the dentist. "And where's the bookkeeper you kidnapped?"

"I didn't kidnap her," Jackson snapped back. "I saved her from a shooter who killed her boss and coworker. And you're going to prison as an accomplice to those murders if you don't talk to me."

Not willing to risk leaning her head out to watch, she bit her lip and glanced around, searching for a better location, one that would ensure she could hear every word—and maybe be in position to help if the dentist tried to pull a gun. Her gaze lowered to the ground. Did she dare?

A teenager stopped at a nearby traffic light, blasting his radio. Bailey hoped the loud music would drown out the sounds she made crawling under the bed of the truck. Hard asphalt and gravel dug into her bare fore-arms as she pulled her body closer to a spot where she could see both men. The overwhelming smell of motor oil assaulted her senses, but she did her best to ignore it and concentrate on the two men.

"I didn't have anything to do with those killings," Dr. York shot back through gritted teeth. He reached for his door handle, clearly ready to skip his morning coffee to escape the confrontation.

Jackson snatched the man's keys with his left hand, leaving his gun hand free. "Your wife's cousin trashed Dr. Daniels's house yesterday and attempted to kill his bookkeeper."

Dr. York's eyes widened in surprise. "That has nothing to do with me. Her cousins are all dolts."

"You have half a dozen drug traffickers coming and going from your dental practice regularly. No one has that many cavities. They belong to the same trafficking ring your wife's cousin is in. The same cousin who broke into Dr. Daniels's house. I don't believe in coincidences."

The dentist paled.

Bailey leaned her head against the truck's heavy-duty tire to get a better look. From her cramped position beneath a ton of metal, she studied the cowboy's stern features, trying to figure him out. From the way he was interrogating the dentist, anyone would think he was a law enforcement officer, not a maintenance guy. Did it come from watching crime dramas every night, or was there something he hadn't told her about his background?

Under Jackson's scrutiny, Dr. York's lips pressed together into a grim line, perhaps resigning himself to the inevitable.

"My wife said they would kill me if I didn't do what they wanted," the dentist admitted. "I think she offered my services to them for money. Lots of money, by the looks of the jewelry she brings home."

"What services?" Jackson pressed. "I need details."

York rubbed his forehead and closed his eyes as if not wanting to admit the truth even to himself.

"You can tell me or the police."

"Okay." The dentist's voice faltered. "I altered the appearance of their teeth. Veneers, caps, even braces. A huge guy covered in tattoos gave me dental X-ray images to add to each of their files. And I was ordered not to take any new X-rays. They're planning to fake their deaths and move their operation out of state or out of the country. I don't know which."

Bailey gaped. Faking their deaths meant other men fitting the same physical description would die in their place, with their identities "proven" by the dental records the tattooed man had supplied.

"These men are ruthless." The dentist hung his head low. "I'm only alive because they need me—and I know that that won't protect me for much longer." He glanced over his shoulder as if confirming he and Jackson were still alone. "I had no clue what I was getting into when I married my wife. And once we had children, it was too late to leave her. I must protect my sons from her family's influence."

Jackson glared at the man. "Why did they kill Dr. Daniels and his receptionist?"

The dentist sighed. "Around a month ago, my wife's cousin asked—*demanded*—I arrange a meeting. They wanted plastic surgery for some celebrity. It had to be kept under wraps so the press wouldn't find out."

Bailey furrowed her brow. *How would a group of thugs know a celebrity?*

A couple of men in suits pulled into a parking space four car lengths away, and Dr. York turned, shielding his face with a hand pressed to his forehead.

Jackson waited for the coffee shop's glass door to close behind the new arrivals before continuing. "Who had the surgery?"

"I don't know. No one volunteered the information, and I knew better than to ask."

"You need to tell the police."

"No." The dentist shook his head vehemently. "They showed me a picture of what happens to people who talk. I'm taking my family out of town until the situation cools off around here. For a month. Maybe longer."

"My brother is a detective. The police already know these guys have been frequenting your practice." Jackson took an intimidating step closer. "Do you want to go to prison?"

"Of course not."

"Then tell me—why did they kill the surgeon? And why do they want his bookkeeper so badly? Give me something to work with. Something to point the police in a different direction."

"Would that keep me out of jail?" York's voice rose with panic.

"It might. But I can tell you one thing. If you decide to clam up now, you're definitely rotting behind bars."

Bailey crawled closer to the edge of the truck, trying to get a better look at the dentist's reaction. A rock scratched her bare arm, and she tightened her fists to push away the sting.

"My wife knows a lot more than she's saying. I'm sure of it." Dr. York dragged his hand through his hair. Worry lines creased his brow, and he stared at the asphalt beneath his feet as if reaching into the far recesses of his mind for an idea. "What if I leave the house unlocked and the alarm turned off when we leave? We'll be gone an hour from now. Maybe sooner. She keeps her password on a note hidden under the keyboard. I own the computer, and she uses a joint email account you can access by clicking on the envelope icon."

"If it's a joint account," Jackson began tentatively, "why haven't you read her emails to see what she's up to?"

Dr. York's face drooped, and he stared at the ground. "I don't want to know the truth."

Jackson handed the man back his keys and walked away. When he rounded the white pickup truck, he knocked on the tailgate. "Let's go, Bailey."

She rolled her eyes and crawled out of her hiding place. Pebbles dug into her arms. While rushing to catch up with him, she brushed away the dirt and gravel clinging to her body and her clothes. She grimaced at the realization that the black stains on her yellow shirt would never come out. "Do you believe him?"

"I do," Jackson tossed over his shoulder. "But I don't trust him." He tugged open the driver's-side door.

"Does that mean we're not going to the dentist's house?" Bailey jumped into her seat.

"*I'm* going to the dentist's house. I'll figure out a way for Cole to keep an eye on you while I'm gone."

"But—"

"I told you to stay put, and you didn't." Jackson turned over the engine. "If I can't trust you to listen to me when it comes to your safety, then I can't bring you into a situation that might turn dangerous. You're not talking me into taking you this time."

"I had a good reason," she mumbled.

He ignored her.

On the drive back to the motel, Bailey wracked her brain, trying to remember if she could have seen this secret celebrity patient in the office.

Her stomach flip-flopped when she noticed an old gray pickup truck parked on the east side of the motel. "We're not alone."

Jackson scanned their surroundings and drove forward with one hand on the wheel, the other hovering near his back holster.

No one jumped out of a room or rushed them from behind a tree. When they neared the truck, he gestured toward it with a jerk of his head. "Those are national park stickers, and that looks like camping gear."

"Meaning the owner is most likely a guest and not a drug trafficker?" she asked, using the term she'd heard Jackson use. He'd never called them traffickers around her. Again, secrets. She hated secrets.

"Probably."

While Jackson drove, she tried to read the names of the parks printed on various colorful decals lining the perimeter of the truck's back window. Large containers, including coolers and what could be a bagged tent, filled the truck bed. "I'm glad our room isn't on this side of the motel."

"We still have to be careful." Jackson continued to eye their surroundings as they rounded the building.

He chose to park between the rooms they had rented and the ones they slept in the previous night. Nothing appeared out of place.

They had less than an hour to wait until the dentist left town with his family. Bailey unlocked the passenger door and got out. Unable to hide her resentment, she said, "I assume you're going to call Cole now and ask him to babysit me."

Instead of answering, Jackson scowled and climbed out of the car.

She shut the passenger-side door and jumped at a loud clicking sound coming from the motel. The door in front of her swung open. A scruffy middle-aged man with an unkempt beard, brandishing a gun with a long barrel, stepped out of a room. He stood about six foot tall in his dirty jeans, short-sleeved plaid shirt and faded baseball cap.

"Put your hands up in the air!" He kept his weapon pointed at Jackson, whose hands reached out to his sides more so than up in the air.

Bailey's breath caught in her throat, and her knees threatened to buckle beneath her as she slowly raised her hands. If Jackson were fast enough, he could reach for the gun holstered behind his back, but then what would happen? *Lord, please don't let this end in a gunfight. Help us escape without anyone dying.*

"Little lady, you get behind me," the bearded man urged. "He's not going to hurt you anymore."

Realization dawned on her. This man wasn't one of the drug traffickers. He must have seen them when they drove up and recognized Jackson from the news stories that claimed he was a kidnapper.

"Mister," she said in a soft, calming voice, "those news reports were wrong. No one kidnapped me."

"This lowlife is forcing you to say that." The bearded man, undeterred, motioned with the gun toward the building. "Sit on the sidewalk while I call the police." He removed a cell phone from his shirt pocket.

Her pulse skipped a beat. This couldn't possibly end well. The lieutenant likely still thought Jackson was a kidnapper. If this guy didn't accidentally shoot him, a trigger-happy police officer might. And if the leak found out their location, they could be dodging bullets from the drug traffickers, too. What could she do? Movie scenarios flashed through her mind.

Jackson met her gaze, as if saying he planned to make a move any second now. He eased toward the sidewalk on the left side of the bearded man.

Bailey approached the man's far-right side, giving Jackson room to act. But she could tell he needed a distraction. She pretended to trip and fell to the asphalt with a squeal.

The gunman whipped around in her direction. Jackson grabbed the weapon out of one hand and knocked the phone out of the other. It landed six feet away with a thwack.

Bailey rushed over to snatch the cell phone, the scratch on her knee stinging with each step. Jackson had turned the bearded man's weapon on him, ready to fire if necessary.

The man's eyes widened with fear. "Are you going to kill me?"

"Not if you cooperate." Jackson took the cell phone from Bailey and threw it far behind the parking lot. The leaves of a bush shook when it bounced off a branch and landed on the red dirt. "Get the duct tape."

She wished they had a second or even third roll. At this rate, they would need an economy pack. Jackson unlocked the room they had rented while she grabbed the tape from the back seat and hurried back.

"Sit in the chair and don't talk," Jackson told the man once they were inside. "Housecleaning starts on this side of the motel soon. They'll free you."

The expression on his face said he didn't know if he should comply with the order. But he had to know that a struggle would most likely end in bloodshed. She prayed that didn't happen.

"No one is going to hurt you," Bailey promised. She held up the tape. "I'll do this. It'll be okay. I promise."

It was immediately apparent when the man decided not to fight against them. He slumped into the chair.

Jackson held the gun on him while she went to work, taping him up. Afraid he might hop over to the window or door, she taped him and the chair to the bed's headboard.

Bailey never dreamed she would ever have to participate in anything like this once, let alone twice in the same twenty-four-hour period. "I'm sorry," she whispered. "But you didn't give us any choice. He really is innocent."

The man furrowed his brow and growled beneath the tape gagging his mouth. Even without words, he made his point clear: they didn't look innocent right now.

Jackson checked to make sure the man couldn't escape, yanked the motel's phone cord from the wall and then gestured for her to leave. "Be patient," he told the bearded man. "Don't do anything foolish. Help will come soon."

After Jackson shut the door, Bailey walked ahead of him to the rooms they had slept in the night before. "I know," she stated before he could say anything. "We need to grab our stuff and go before it's too late."

As Jackson drove, he scanned the multi-million dollar homes for an inconspicuous parking place near Dr. York's address. The spacious properties certainly seemed grander than Jackson would have expected from a dentist's salary. Once Martinez and Steele took a deep dive into the dentist's financials, they may discover he had been working for the drug traffickers much longer than suspected.

Bailey sat in the passenger seat with a self-satisfied expression on her face. She knew he had no choice but to take her with him. With Cole busy dealing with the bearded man back at the motel, he couldn't watch her. He couldn't ask the other agents to watch her—not without telling her that he was with the DEA.

"We can park on the shoulder of the road up ahead," she suggested. "It will look like we're hiking or taking pictures of the scenery."

Impressed, Jackson glanced over at her. "Are you sure you're not a private detective?"

"I solve every crime when I watch a mystery for the second time."

A smile tugged at his lips as he pulled over onto the dirt shoulder diagonally across from the house. Dr. York's closed blinds and empty driveway gave the impression he had indeed taken his family out of town.

Jackson didn't trust appearances. He studied the

shrubbery and trees around them for signs of movement from someone waiting to ambush them. When he felt comfortable leaving the car, he pushed open his door. "We're good to go."

She joined him at the edge of the residential road and blocked the sun from her eyes with the side of her hand. "I heard Dr. York say he would leave the front door unlocked and the alarm turned off."

"Let's hope he told the truth." Jackson placed his hand protectively on her shoulder. "Stick close to me and keep your eyes open. I don't want a repeat of what happened in Dr. Daniels's garage."

He felt her grow tense beneath his touch. At least she took his warning seriously.

They walked past an ornate water fountain and beneath a stone arch on the way to the front door. When no one answered the bell, he turned the knob. It opened. Silence greeted them. His senses sharpened with each step he took inside the spacious living room.

Bailey pulled the door shut behind them.

A large flat-screen television hung over a decorative fireplace mantel on the far wall, and modular dark brown leather furniture took up most of the room. Jackson stood still, listening. Convinced they were alone, he glanced into the kitchen and dining room before pointing toward the hall. "We need to work fast."

"I'm guessing we'll be able to tell which is her computer area because it will have more color than his," Bailey whispered. "But I could be wrong."

He appreciated the way she proactively thought through situations. It might save them time here. Despite his misgivings, he'd come to think of her as a partner of sorts. But an actual DEA partner would have the self-defense training to protect herself. He'd have to remember that that was something Bailey lacked. As smart and capable as she was, he still needed to make sure to keep her safe,

They crept down a hallway, past two children's rooms and a linen closet, before they found a meticulously organized office. Two computer monitors occupied the corner of the mahogany desk.

"This is Dr. York's office." She lifted a book on orthodontia to show him the cover and then returned it to the accent table next to an overstuffed chair.

"Let's try the room across the hall." When he spotted photographs of Paris hanging on the wall in ornate frames, his gut told him they had found Mrs. York's office.

Bailey lifted a purple throw pillow from a chaise longue. "Color."

"I never doubted you." Behind the white L-shaped desk, Jackson located the password tucked under the computer keyboard. "This is it."

With a touch of a button, he booted up the computer and entered *Paris2025*. He sat in the executive leather chair and pulled up Mrs. York's emails. It didn't take long to find a thread of correspondence between her and Karl, the cousin who'd tried to strangle Bailey. His email address included his first name. No one could accuse him of being a criminal mastermind.

Bailey placed her hand on his shoulder and leaned closer to read aloud. "She's recovered from the surgery and leaving the country next Friday."

Jackson found it difficult to focus with her standing so close and touching him. "I'm not finding who *she* is, but I'm guessing this is our celebrity client."

"I doubt she's a celebrity in the true sense of the word. A drug ring wouldn't help an actress get a face-lift. She's probably someone they consider important enough to hide her true identity from—"

"Law enforcement," he stated with absolute confidence. "These guys are planning to fake their deaths to disappear. This woman is changing her appearance to keep authorities from arresting her."

"Or following her?" Bailey shifted to the side and gazed down at him. The golden flecks in her brown eyes sparkled as she continued her train of thought. "They'll have to go somewhere after they fake their deaths. The police must know her connection to these guys for her to go to such lengths to disguise her."

"Her connection might be to the kingpin. I was told he fled the country when his right-hand man and a few henchmen were arrested in Phoenix." There Jackson went again, stretching the truth and hating every second. Bailey would assume that he'd been told by Cole— but actually, it had been Jackson's supervisor.

The task force position was looking better every day. Jackson continued, "This so-called celebrity could be leaving the country to meet up with the big boss."

Bailey tapped a glittery purple pen on the desk with her fingernail. "Could this kingpin have replaced the right-hand man with a woman?"

He shrugged. "It's possible."

They both jumped at the sound of car tires.

Jackson peered out through a slit in the window blinds. Two police cruisers had pulled into the dentist's driveway. His pulse raced. "We have company."

NINE

Bailey gripped the back of the chair with both hands. "Who's out there?"

"The police." Jackson shut down the computer and hurried out from behind the desk. "Let's go."

Her pulse raced faster than her feet as they ran down the hall and into the kitchen. She headed toward the sliding glass door but noticed Jackson veered off in another direction.

"They'll be watching the back exit," he whispered and opened the garage door with a gentle twist of the knob, revealing two black luxury cars. He snatched two key rings off a set of hooks hanging on the wall.

A resounding knock at the front door made Bailey jolt, and her stomach flip-flopped. "Hurry." She kept her voice low and waved her hands rapidly to urge him forward.

Jackson lifted a finger to his lips. They slipped into the dimly lit garage and gently closed the door behind them. He positioned his thumbs over both fobs, and another round of knocking drowned out the clicking of the trunk locks.

"Police! Anyone here?" The officer's voice boomed through the space.

Bailey cringed. *I should have locked the front door after we came in.*

Jackson swiftly opened the trunk of the closest vehicle, shoved a gym bag to the side and motioned for her to climb in.

She shook her head no. He had to be kidding. The small, cramped quarters smelled like a pile of sweaty socks. There had to be a better place to hide. She pointed toward the cabinets. If Mrs. York's cousin could hide in one, she could, too.

Jackson glared at her.

The patrol officers' shoes clicked on the tile inside the house. She panicked. Her fear of going to jail for capturing the man at the motel outweighed her disgust at the thought of smelling like a football team's locker room. She climbed inside as quietly as possible.

Jackson waited for her to curl into a fetal position before lowering the trunk's lid and shutting out the light.

With her heart pounding in her ears, she peered into the darkness, straining to hear Jackson walk over to the other car and hide in its trunk, but silence filled the small space. The carpet below her bare arms felt rough to the touch.

A loud sweeping sound signaled the opening of the door leading from the kitchen into the garage. Her breath caught in her throat. Why hadn't she immediately crawled inside the trunk? If Jackson were caught and arrested because he didn't have time to hide, it would be her fault.

A heavy set of footsteps on the concrete floor grew

louder and closer. The officer walked around the car, pausing every few seconds. The nearby cabinets creaked and banged one at a time.

God, I know I don't deserve your mercy. Please, forgive me for my sins and help us out of this situation.

An eternity passed before the kitchen door closed, and the footsteps faded away.

Bailey felt so alone without Jackson, whom she'd come to depend on. She rubbed the pendant dangling from her necklace and sighed.

Both the police and drug traffickers were after them now. How would she ever get home?

The heavy front door shut with a loud thud, and the faint sound of male voices outside carried into the garage. The officers would leave soon, but she suspected Jackson would wait until the cruisers drove away to free her.

The foul-smelling air grew thick, forcing her to inhale with shallow breaths. It seemed as if the moment she couldn't take it any longer, engines roared outside, and Jackson popped open her trunk.

Bailey climbed out with his help and then threw her arms around him. His solid, broad shoulders offered the sense of security she craved. "That was too close."

He gave her a quick hug, then stepped back, his hands sliding down to her forearms. His eyes were warm and caring. "I agree."

That brief spark of connection between them, along with the ability to stretch her legs and breathe again, eased her anxiety. She preferred the aroma of car grease over dirty socks any day. "What now?" she asked, still afraid to raise her voice to a normal speaking level.

He held up his cell phone. "I order flowers."

* * *

Jackson peered through a slit in the living room blinds and found the driveway empty. A quick check of the property convinced him they were alone. "They're gone."

"Are you positive?" Bailey seemed poised to run back to the garage.

"For now." He was under no illusions that they'd be able to stay hidden for long. The whole world seemed to be after them. It was bad enough the drug ring wanted her dead. Now that Jackson's face was plastered all over the news, he feared someone might shoot at him and accidentally hit Bailey. There were too many ways for things to go disastrously wrong.

A few minutes later, they walked into the dining room together, and Bailey asked, "What did you mean earlier when you said you were ordering flowers?"

"I have a plan. I'm guessing one of the neighbors spotted us entering the house. Someone who knows the dentist left town. If we walk back to the car, that same neighbor could call the police again. We need alternate transportation out of here."

"Your plan involves flowers?"

"A florist," he explained, leading her to sit on the cushioned seats at the mahogany dining table.

Dialing the number he'd known all his life, he let out a sigh of relief when the florist shop's phone was answered by his mother's best friend. "Pearl, this is Jackson. Don't say my name. No one else can know you're talking to me."

"Yes, I can help you with that," she responded in her pleasant, professional manner.

"I'm sure you've seen me on the news, but I promise you none of it's true."

"Of course," she answered, her voice unwavering. "I would stake my reputation on it."

Relief lifted his mood. "I need a favor, but if you're not comfortable with it, I understand."

"Anything for one of my favorite customers. How many red roses would you like?"

"Thank you." He knew he could depend on her. Their families had been tight through thick and thin. "We need to hide out in that rental home you were planning to renovate," he said, then added step-by-step instructions on how to sneak them out of the dentist's house and transport them to the safe house before disconnecting the call.

Bailey pushed a strand of her silky, dark hair behind her ear. "You're positive you can trust this woman?"

"Pearl's like a second mother. She even sent me to my room for time-out once." He smiled at the memory. "I was a bratty five-year-old."

"I was, too. Something else we have in common." Their gazes locked for a brief moment. "How long will it take her to get here?"

"Ten minutes. We'll need to be ready in eight."

"The stress of the past couple of days is getting to me." Bailey left the table and curled up on the sofa in the great room off the kitchen, where she rubbed her pendant. "Do you think I'll ever go home again?"

He stepped closer and lifted her chin with a finger. Looking directly into her sad eyes, he promised, "Yes, you will go home again. And soon."

She reached up and placed her hand over his. "Thank you. I needed to hear that."

His heart warmed at her touch, giving more strength to his growing feelings for her. It was a struggle to remember to let his training take over, but once he did, his mind quickly compartmentalized his emotions. He turned away and settled into a wingback chair, where he avoided eye contact until she spoke again.

"I'm worried about my father. He needs me."

"Sounds like you two are close."

She nodded, continuing to rub her pendant. "He raised me after my mother left us. I was only two. I don't think he ever got over it, even if he says he forgave her."

Jackson had his own troubles with forgiveness after what he'd seen in his line of work. "That had to be hard on you, too. Every kid needs their mother." He'd been raised by a loving woman who went the extra mile to ensure her children were healthy and happy. He couldn't imagine his life without her.

"Forgiveness was easier for me because I barely remember her," Bailey shared. "Don't get me wrong—there were times when I was angry or resentful. Who leaves their kid and never calls once to see how she's doing? To this day, I have no clue where she lives. But then my dad explained that she had mental health issues. It wasn't my fault or his that she left. She was doing the best she could under the circumstances."

Jackson blew out a breath. He was impressed. "You have to be the most well-adjusted person I've ever met."

"I wouldn't go that far." She grabbed a red throw pillow and hugged it to her chest. "I have issues just like everyone else."

"Oh?" It dawned on him to wonder why she was in her thirties and unmarried. A woman so kind and beautiful should have been scooped up long ago. "Is your mother the reason you're still single?"

She flinched, appearing stricken. Jackson wanted to take the question back, but she answered before he could. "No. I've dated. Nothing serious until three summers ago. Rod asked me to marry him, and I said yes."

"Is he the former fiancé you mentioned before?"

Bailey pressed her lips into a thin line and nodded. "I left him when I discovered he had a girlfriend on the side."

"I am so sorry." And he meant that sincerely. "The man was a fool."

"No, I was." She sighed, and embarrassment flickered across her face. "The first time I caught him cheating, he pointed out that we'd only been dating for a few months and said we had never discussed dating exclusively. Then he said that if I wanted to take that giant step, he was ready to commit."

Jackson had met men like Rod before. They couldn't be trusted. "A few months seems long enough to assume you were exclusive, but that's just me."

"Me, too. Long story short, I figured it was my fault for assuming the state of our relationship and agreed to date exclusively. A year later, he popped the question. I said yes."

"Then…"

"I showed up one day at his house unannounced and found him in a compromising position with his former girlfriend. He dared to tell me it wasn't what it looked like. I didn't say a word. Instead, I dropped my ring in his fish tank on the way out the door."

Jackson started to speak, but she lifted a finger to stop him. "It gets even better. I soon discovered someone had been charging items on my credit card for an entire month. He'd bought her gifts and shipped them to her address."

"That's horrible."

"It truly is my fault for not trusting my instincts and calling things off after the first time I caught him cheating. He lied, and I let him convince me that I should give him the benefit of the doubt. I'll never make that mistake again."

Guilt washed over Jackson like a tsunami. "I don't blame you for protecting your heart. At least you have your father. There are people out there who don't have anyone to care about them."

Bailey touched her pendant. "I know. I'm blessed."

She deserved more than Jackson could give her, but he resolved that for whatever time they had together, he would be as open as he could. He wanted her to know him—the real Jackson Walker, regardless of whether she ever wanted a relationship with him. "My family's close, but I've never had to take care of any of them like you do your father. I have two older brothers, so they looked after both me and our younger sister, Lily, when our parents were busy."

The stress lines on her forehead faded away now that the conversation had shifted to his life. "Did your parents both work?" she asked.

"They own a horse ranch my father inherited from his parents. It's my favorite place in the entire world. I have fond memories of my grandfather teaching me how to ride and my grandmother planting strawberries with me at her side. I was her little helper."

Bailey sighed. "I always loved horses. My father used to take me to a stable outside of town on Saturday mornings for riding lessons. The owners had a gorgeous green house with flowers blooming in boxes under the front windows."

He beamed with pride. "Sounds like our place."

"Small world." The warmth in her eyes revealed her pleasure at their newfound connection. "I remember a tall cowboy teaching the lesson."

"That would have been my father. On Saturdays, my brothers and I helped my grandfather lead trail rides."

A smile brightened her face. "I think I remember you. Do your brothers both have darker hair?"

"They do." Jackson's heart tugged at the idea that they had spent time together as children. He glanced at the clock on the wall and jumped up. He wished they could talk more. There was so much to learn about Bailey Scott, but it would have to wait for another time. If it ever came. "Let's head out back."

TEN

Bailey hid with Jackson behind the York family's back-yard gate. They didn't dare speak as they waited. She glanced down at the cowboy hat he held in his hands. He rarely took it off when outside. Maybe he feared it would be seen over the gate. After all, he was a tall man. A tall, handsome man.

She shifted her focus away from Jackson and back to the street. The way he harbored secrets reminded her of Rod. There'd been signs she had ignored with her former fiancé. Evening business calls he took outside. Long stretches of time when he didn't return her texts. Last-minute changes of plans without good excuses.

Jackson kept his life private, building an emotional wall around himself. She didn't think he was hiding a girlfriend, but it was almost worse because he was hiding his true self. And yet he'd knocked off a few bricks for her today. She could only guess what that meant. Did he want to be friends? Or something more? She could handle friendship. The wall would have to tumble down before she could risk anything else.

A full minute passed before the hum of an engine drew near. Bailey peered through a slit in the wooden gate and watched a Pearl's Flowers van back into the driveway. The green vehicle rolled to a stop six feet short of the garage door.

Seconds ticked by before a short woman with shoulder-length silver hair wearing an apron emblazoned with the store's logo walked around to the back of the van. She tugged the doors wide open and reached inside for a long white box decorated with a red satin bow.

When she headed toward the front door with the order of long-stemmed roses, Jackson gestured for Bailey to follow him. Their escape plan depended on Pearl distracting nosy neighbors, if any were watching, while Bailey and Jackson slipped through the gate and into the back of the van. Jackson tossed his hat inside the van, climbed in and reached out his hand to help her.

Here we go again, Bailey thought before crawling in with him. They scooted far away from the doors and leaned against one side. At least they were able to sit and stretch their legs instead of curling up in a trunk.

The florist returned with the box after no one answered the front door. Pearl winked at Jackson, then offered Bailey a smile while she shoved the delivery off to the side. When she slammed the doors shut, darkness enveloped them, and a lock clicked into place. Bailey searched for a window, but there wasn't one. Her breath hitched. She didn't usually have issues with claustrophobia, but sitting in a small, dark compartment for who knows how long made her uncomfortable.

"We're safe." Jackson stretched his arm around her shoulders, pulling her close to his side.

Bailey nestled into him as if she had done so a hundred times before. His masculine scent mingled with the aroma of flowers, and her body relaxed. The van's engine coming to life broke the silence, and they moved forward before bouncing over the curb.

Jackson ran his hand over her arm, reassuring her that all was well. They traveled several miles before he spoke. "Feeling any better?"

"I am. Thank you." She lifted her head off his shoulder. "How long will it take to reach Pearl's rental house?"

"About twenty minutes."

Before Bailey could follow up on that question, another thought popped into her mind. "What about your car?"

"I'll have someone pick it up later."

"Oh." Thinking about spending another twenty minutes in the dark sent goose bumps traveling down her arms.

The van took a corner too fast, and they leaned into the turn. About five minutes later, Jackson broke the silence. "Can I ask you a question?"

His serious tone worried her. "Is there something wrong?"

"No. Well, nothing you don't already know. You've mentioned praying a few times, which got me thinking about God. I've had trouble forgiving people for several years now. Do you mind continuing our discussion from inside the house?"

"I'm no counselor or religious expert."

"You've got experience with the subject. That's good enough for me."

"What do you want to know?" she answered, her voice still uncertain.

He hesitated before asking, "Did you forgive your former fiancé?"

Her stomach clenched.

He blew out an exasperated breath. "I'm sorry. I shouldn't have asked."

"It's okay." She was the one who had mentioned her ex inside the house. "I did forgive Rod, but I haven't forgotten what he did."

Jackson tensed beside her. "So if another man lied to you but had a good reason, you wouldn't forgive him?"

"I wouldn't date a man in the first place unless he was open and completely honest with me."

If only she could see Jackson's face, try to read his expression. Was he referring to himself when he asked about a man who lied for a good reason? If so, she was glad that he now knew they had no chance of a relationship unless he stopped hiding behind his secrets.

"While we're on the topic…" He paused long enough to make her curiosity grow. "Do you ever think you'll forgive the man who shot Amy and Dr. Daniels?"

Her eyes widened in surprise.

"I don't think I could," he continued. "I've seen some horrible things in my life. I don't understand man's inhumanity to man. I can't make sense of why God gave man free will, knowing this would happen. I eventually stopped going to church. I guess that's why I'm asking you the tough questions."

"I believe God gave us free will so it would be our choice to love Him and to accept Him into our hearts. When we sin and repent, His forgiveness is a gift." She reached deep inside for an honest answer regarding how she felt about the shooter. "I wish I could say I've already forgiven the masked man, but I'm not sure if I ever will. I hope I can. One day. After many prayers. Forgiveness frees the person who does the forgiving, and that freedom is something I want, even if it's not easy to achieve." Had she truly forgiven Rod? If not, was that the reason she had trouble moving on to a new relationship?

"The fact you want to forgive the shooter says a lot about your character." His matter-of-fact tone told her he meant every word.

"I like to think it says more about the power of God."

"I vote for both." A pause hung in the darkness. "I started praying again since I've met you."

"That's good." She waited for him to continue, but he fell silent. She understood his reluctance. A relationship with God was personal.

The van suddenly started bouncing, and it felt like they were now driving over an unpaved road.

She planted both hands on the floor, trying to keep from falling over.

"I do believe Pearl is driving over the back road to my family's ranch," Jackson explained.

Fear gripped her. "That wasn't the plan. The lieutenant thinks you kidnapped me. Wouldn't he expect you to go home to your family?"

"Pearl wouldn't take us to the ranch unless my parents instructed her to do so—and they wouldn't have done that unless they were sure it was safe. My father has a drone. He would know if the ranch is under any surveillance."

Bailey wasn't convinced. They could be walking— or driving—into a trap. "What do we do if the police stop the van before it reaches the house?"

"Pray. And follow my lead."

When the van's back doors opened, Jackson found his father, dressed, as usual, in jeans and a long-sleeved plaid shirt. He stood with his hands on his hips, waiting for them beneath the cover of trees shading the backyard. The worry lines stretched across his face, from one graying temple to the other, softened.

"About time you got here. I can't believe you thought it would be better to hide out in an empty rental house without a stick of furniture inside. And don't tell me you were protecting us from danger. *Every member of the Walker family can take care of themselves.*" He reached for Bailey's hand to help her out. "I'm Hank, Jackson's father," he said in a kinder voice. "Welcome to our home."

Jackson grabbed his hat and shook off the admonishment. He had spent most of his life trying to impress his father the way his brothers seemed to do with ease. It was one of the reasons he'd become a DEA agent. Hiding in the back of a van was not how he'd wanted to return home. "Thanks for taking us in," he said, crawling out behind Bailey.

"That's what family's for. Remember that the next time you need a place to hide out. If there is a next time." His father scowled. "Now, get yourself inside."

The tension between Jackson's shoulders eased when he took in his family's two-story home and spotted his mother rushing out the kitchen door. She was wearing boots with her light blue cotton dress. That meant she'd been out to the chicken coop. Otherwise, she'd be wearing her "comfortable" shoes.

Jackson placed his hand onto Bailey's back to guide her as they walked past the expansive porch held up by decorative pillars.

His mother hugged him tightly. "I am so glad you're

home and unharmed." She stepped back to give him a once-over. "Not a scratch on you. Thank the Lord."

"I'm fine. Mom, this is Bailey."

She took Bailey's hands in her own. "Are you hungry, dear?"

"Maybe after the butterflies settle, Mrs. Walker," Bailey said, touching her stomach.

"That's understandable. You've been through so much." Jackson was sure that his mother's gentle tone would go a long way in making Bailey feel welcome. "And please, call me Elise." She ushered their guest into the kitchen. "I'll show you to your room, and then you can shower and rest before we eat."

"I don't have a change of clothes." Bailey sounded apologetic.

His mother pushed strands of her shoulder-length blond hair behind her ear. "No worries. Our daughter, Lily, will have something you can wear."

"I don't want to put anyone out."

"You're not, dear."

In the kitchen, Jackson grabbed a water bottle from the stainless steel refrigerator and handed it to Bailey. "Drink up. You don't want to get dehydrated."

Bailey sent him one of her heartwarming smiles. He took it in but then caught his mother studying him with a hopeful expression lighting up her face. Embarrassed, he turned away to snatch another water bottle for himself, then followed his father past the kitchen island on the way to the dining room. He sat in a fabric-covered chair at the same wooden table where he'd shared countless family meals, and a comforting sense of familiarity took hold.

His father sat across from him and frowned. "I spoke

to Cole. Looks like you've gotten yourself into quite a pickle."

Jackson sighed. "You could say things went from bad to worse."

"I just did. From what I hear on the news, you're a wanted man."

"I'm hoping Cole will straighten that out soon." Jackson placed his hat on the table and ran his hand through his hair. "Bailey never told her father I kidnapped her."

"The reporter is lying?"

"Or the leak in the police department lied to the reporter."

"I see." Deep lines fanned out from his father's dark eyes. "What do you need from us?"

"A place to lay low and get some rest and some food." The aroma of simmering beef and vegetables permeating the air made his stomach rumble. "Mom making stew?"

"She is."

As if on cue, his mother returned from showing Bailey the guest room. "She's a lovely girl, Jackson."

"Who thinks I'm a handyman."

She smiled at her husband, her way of telling him she hoped there might be more to Jackson's relationship with Bailey.

"Mom, I'm working. My job is to keep Bailey safe, not date her."

She patted his hand. "That won't be your job forever."

His younger sister, Lily, appeared from the hallway, her straight, long blond hair hanging over one shoulder. "Bailey seems nice."

"She is," Jackson agreed. "And smart. And attractive. And a case I'm working on, so all of you can stop trying to play matchmaker."

"I wasn't going to until you just made it clear you like her." Lily chuckled, showing off her perfect teeth.

His mother glanced up at her. "Bailey doesn't know he's more than a handyman," she whispered.

"If you like her, then you should tell her," his sister suggested.

"It's not that simple." After their discussion in the van, he was positive Bailey wouldn't have room in her heart for him if she discovered his deception. She would forgive but not forget. And there was still her safety to consider.

"Maybe it is that simple." Lily turned to their mother. "When I heard Jackson was heading this way, I rescheduled the riding lessons I was giving for next week. I have time on my hands. Need help in the kitchen?"

"I do." Her gaze traveled between her son and husband as she stood. "You two figure out how to solve this mess while we're gone."

"Yes, ma'am," Jackson answered. He hated that his sister had to send away paying customers. He'd make it up to his family once the traffickers were behind bars. And more than just financially. It wasn't beneath him to roll up his sleeves and muck out a stall or mend a fence.

His father waited for the women to slip into the kitchen before speaking. "Cole shared the details of the shooting. What I don't know is why you're still the one protecting Bailey."

Jackson filled him in on how they were attacked on the way to the hotel's safe room and what his supervisor had to say.

"Your boss is right about one thing—she is better off

with you than anyone else. But why continue to hide behind the handyman job? Doesn't she deserve to know who you really are?"

His father's confidence in him meant the world to Jackson, but thinking about the past made him swallow hard. "I can't tell Bailey. I made that mistake once. I won't do it again."

"What happened?" His father tilted his head, studying him.

Jackson had never told the story to anyone outside of the DEA, but he had the sense that now was the time. He wanted his father to understand. "A few years ago, I worked undercover on an estate owned by the head of a drug cartel. He had a niece visiting there during her college's spring break. She was an innocent about to end up in the middle of a raid. I was afraid she would be shot in the crossfire."

His father leaned closer. "What did you do?"

"I told her she should leave early to beat the heavy traffic expected that weekend. She said she didn't mind traffic. Then I told her the situation within her uncle's import business was getting messier every day, and she should leave before trouble broke out. She said her uncle and her father would handle everything. She had no clue they were both smuggling drugs."

"You must have been ready to hog-tie her and throw her in the trunk of your car."

"I wish I had." Regret weighed heavily on Jackson's mind. "Eight hours before the raid, I broke down and told her I was a DEA agent, that her uncle's money came from drug trafficking and that if she wanted to live, she had to leave within the hour. The last time I saw her alive, she was running back to her room to pack."

His father gaped. "The last time you saw her *alive*?"

Jackson nodded, feeling the guilt twist in his stomach at the memory. "She called a friend to tell her she was heading back to school that day and why. One of her uncle's men was walking down the hall. He overheard and reported the conversation. Her uncle suspected she had become a DEA informant. He executed her in front of her parents. He was convicted of her murder, but that didn't bring the girl back."

"Whoa." His father sat back in his chair, his expression turning thoughtful. "Son, it's not your fault that girl died."

"It feels like it's my fault." He looked directly into his father's eyes. "Since that day, my biggest fear is that someone I care about will be harmed because of my job as an agent. Bailey's facing so much danger already. I don't want to do anything that might make it worse."

His father rubbed his chin. "I understand why you don't want to tell Bailey you're an agent. But the way I see it, if you ever want to settle down, you'll need to share your secret with someone. It's obvious you like this woman. Only you know how deep your feelings for her run and what you're willing to do about it."

ELEVEN

After a long, hot bath, Bailey felt almost normal again. Jackson's family had been so hospitable, even though she had inadvertently pulled them into the danger she was facing. She hoped her presence here wouldn't land them in serious trouble.

Before heading out the guest room door, she glanced in the mirror one last time. Lily's jeans and white blouse fit her perfectly. Jackson's sister had been gracious and understanding, just like his mother. Jackson was fortunate to have a close family. Bailey loved her father, but she'd always secretly wished she had siblings, especially a sister.

On the way to the living room, she admired the large collection of family photos on the walls. One featuring four children on horseback in a grassy field caught her interest.

Jackson turned the corner and blocked the exit from the hall with his broad shoulders. He'd changed into black jeans and a short-sleeved shirt, but the gun remained in the waist holster behind his right hip. "I'm the short kid with the missing front tooth," he said, pointing to the frame on the wall.

Her gaze traveled between the cute towheaded boy in the photograph and the ruggedly handsome man standing in front of her. "How old were you?"

"Seven. Lily was five, Cole ten and Zach twelve. We were playing hide-and-seek with one of my sister's dolls. My brothers were always adapting games for horseback. I hated the way they bossed me around, but we did have fun."

"I would have loved to grow up on a ranch." She shot him a smile. "Does Zach live nearby?"

"His bedroom is directly behind you." Jackson gestured toward the closed door. "Right now, he's on a rare vacation, visiting a friend in Colorado. He manages the ranch with my father and does a lot of search and rescue work as needed."

"Busy man." She admired a family portrait taken on the back porch at least a decade ago. "And Lily? What does she do?"

"Trail rides and private lessons."

"Not involved in serving the community like your brothers?" Bailey asked, tickled by the little girl's toothy smile in the photograph.

An expression she couldn't name flashed across his face. "Lily helps if there's a search for a missing hiker." He crossed his arms over his chest, then rubbed his chin with a thumb as if debating whether he should say something. "Bailey?"

"Yes?"

"When all this is over. I need…" He stopped to clear his throat. "I'd like to talk to you. There are things I want to tell you, but I can't right now."

From his grim expression, she guessed *that* conversation wouldn't end well. Still, it wasn't like she could refuse to hear him out. Not when she owed him so much. "Okay…"

Jackson's mother poked her head into the hall. "There you are. I set out a vegetable tray to hold you over until lunch is ready in about fifteen minutes. I'm sure you must be starving."

Bailey's stomach growled at the mention of food. "Let me help you. I know my way around a kitchen."

His mother waved away the suggestion. "Don't even think about lifting a finger in this house. You are our guest."

"Thank you again. I don't know what we would have done without you." Bailey glanced up at Jackson, hoping he hadn't taken offense, given that coming here hadn't exactly been his idea.

"She's right," he said. "Thank you." He bent to kiss his mother on the forehead.

Mrs. Walker patted her son on the shoulder and then led him and Bailey through the main living space. Upon reaching the dining room table, his mother left them to work in the kitchen.

His father stood. "I need to return a call. I trust you two can manage to stay out of trouble while I'm gone."

"We'll do our best." Jackson pulled out the chair next to him for Bailey. While she filled a small plate with celery and carrots from the vegetable tray, he booted up the laptop he'd left on the table.

She glanced at the silver keyboard. "That looks like the computer we left in the trunk of your car. But it can't be the same laptop."

"It's my old one." The cursor danced over the screen with his quick movements. "I still have a room here, with lots of my stuff." Jackson clicked on a file, and a dozen photographs popped open. "Let me know if you've seen any of these people before."

Bailey leaned closer and caught the aroma of a woodsy aftershave. The scent fit him. Forcing her attention back to the pictures, she realized they were all taken at a party. Purple streamers hung from a ceiling, and wrapped presents covered a table in the corner of the room. Most of the attendees smiled, but not at the camera. "How did you get these?"

"Connections. Do you recognize anyone?"

"Give me a minute." She studied each person's features carefully. Zeroing in on the fifth photograph, she pointed to a familiar face. "That's the guy who attacked me in Dr. Daniels's garage."

"Good." He jotted down notes on a piece of paper. "Anyone else?"

"This was the guy who attacked you in the apartment parking lot." She eyed Jackson speculatively. "These are surveillance pictures, aren't they? Did your brother give you access to them?"

"Something like that."

Bailey didn't press him to explain. Experience had taught her that he would only change the subject. Several photographs later, she felt confusion and disbelief take hold. "The woman in the red dress."

Jackson pointed to the correct picture. "This one?"

Bailey nodded. "She's the woman who showed up for that early-morning consult we talked about."

"Are you positive?"

"Yes. Do you think she's the drug ring's so-called celebrity?"

"If she had a meeting with Daniels, then yes. Do

you remember seeing the name Victoria Hill on any paperwork?"

"No. And if I had seen it, I would have remembered it. I have a great-aunt named Victoria. She must have used a fake identity, which wouldn't be too difficult, since none of the bills would have gone through her insurance companies. Most of them don't cover most cosmetic surgeries. Plus, we offer...*offered* discounts for patients who paid up front with cash."

Jackson's gaze locked with hers. "Think carefully. Do you remember seeing anyone who might have been Victoria after the surgery was performed? For her post-op follow-up, she would have had another early or late appointment to avoid other patients."

Bailey tore her attention away from his deep blue eyes to study the picture. "I don't remember seeing her again, but that's not unusual. I don't really interact with the patients much. It was a fluke that I met her that one time."

Jackson placed his hand over Bailey's as if sharing his strength. "The woman in this photograph is the king-pin's daughter. Her daddy isn't someone you want to cross. He most likely arranged for the hit on the doctor."

"But why?" Bailey's voice hitched with the question. "If she was the so-called celebrity and Dr. Daniels performed the surgery they wanted, then why kill him—and Amy, too?"

"My guess is to protect Victoria's new identity. The shooter must have planted the virus on the computer to destroy any file the doctor might have had on the procedures he performed—anything that might help the authorities, or her father's enemies, figure out her new appearance." Jackson took Bailey's hand in his, a tender move she didn't expect but could grow used to, if she let her guard down.

Jackson continued, "They want to eliminate anyone who might know what she looks like now."

Bailey's stomach performed a somersault. "But I don't know what she looks like now. And all of the doctor's files would have been destroyed by the computer virus."

Jackson ran a finger over his chin. "Maybe not. Would he have performed the surgery if she refused to have before-and-after pictures taken?"

"I doubt it. He insisted on pictures to protect himself from malpractice claims." She lifted her brows. "What are you thinking?"

"The kid in the doctor's garage said he was looking for a thumb drive. And you said yourself that the doctor would have backed up his files somewhere. The question is…where? And who would he have told? His wife definitely doesn't sound like an option, but what about his nurse? Or maybe a close friend?"

Before Bailey could respond, a familiar male voice sounded from the kitchen, along with the clack of boots striking tile. Seconds later, Cole entered the dining room, wearing a grim expression.

Jackson pushed away from the table to meet him halfway. "You've looked better. Please tell me there isn't a SWAT team outside, ready to take me in."

"Not yet, but I heard the lieutenant plans on making a surprise visit here after his meeting with the mayor. So far, you're officially listed as a person of interest, and there's no warrant, but he'll keep his eyes open while pretending to update Mom and Dad on the investigation. I would make myself scarce before he shows up."

"How long do I have?"

"About two hours." Cole took a chair across from Bailey and ran a hand through his dark hair. Having met more of the family, Bailey could now see that he had his father's brown eyes while Jackson had their mother's blue ones. "How are you doing?"

"Okay, I guess." Even though she was worried about the answer he might give, she had to ask: "Are we in trouble for tying up the guy who tried to make a citizen's arrest?"

"No." Cole shook his head. "He admitted he held Jackson at gunpoint even after you told him there was no kidnapping. I reminded the lieutenant that our district attorney would never touch such a weak case."

"It's my fault your lieutenant has it out for Jackson." Bailey glanced up at the cowboy, who had returned to his seat next to her.

"You didn't know what would happen when you called your father." Jackson placed his hand over hers until Cole cleared his throat.

She missed his touch when he pulled away.

"Bailey," Cole said, "I need your father to take my calls from the police department so that I can clear Jackson's name. Do you have any idea how I can make that happen?"

"I'm sure he doesn't trust anyone since the reporter lied." Bailey huffed a breath and considered several possibilities. She had a feeling Jackson and Cole would both say it wasn't safe for her to make a call herself, even from a burner phone, so her options were limited. "You could play him a recording of my voice. That might work."

"It's worth a try." Cole prepped his smart phone and

held it out to her. "What do you want to tell your father?"

"Dad…" Bailey missed him so much she choked on the word. After clearing her throat, she continued, "I love you, and I know you're worried—but right now, I need you to call the police department and tell them Jackson didn't kidnap me. What that reporter said is causing a lot of trouble. A guy held a gun on Jackson. He could have been killed. I need him to protect me so I can come home to you. Please, do it now."

Cole stopped recording and messed with his phone.

"You did a great job." Jackson ran his hand over her forearm.

She swiped away her tears as her gaze locked on his. "I hope it works. I don't want anything bad to happen to you because of me."

After lunch, Jackson excused himself to make a phone call to his supervisor. He called from his childhood room, and as the phone rang, he drank in the nostalgia of being surrounded by collections of baseball cards and comic books. He hoped to pass them down to a child of his own one day. The solid blue comforter on the queen-size bed and oil paintings of wild horses on the walls reflected his current tastes. While leaning against the chair behind his simple black computer desk, he committed to coming home more often. And not just because Bailey lived in Sedona. He'd also look into that task force position.

Mike answered with a curt, "Talk to me."

"Bailey remembers seeing Victoria Hill in Dr. Daniels's office. I believe she's had cosmetic surgery, and the shooting was meant to protect her new identity."

"That's an interesting development." Mike blew out a soft whistle. "I didn't expect that."

"Neither did I," Jackson said as he took a step back and sat on the edge of his bed. "Everyone always made it clear that neither Victoria nor her brother, Anthony, had any desire to take over the family business. The last I heard, he owned a motorcycle shop in Phoenix and she was taking college classes."

"Hang on." A long silence followed before Mike spoke again. "Her financial records show that Victoria rented a house between Sedona and Cottonwood in late December." He rattled off an address. "It looks like she's been temping as a secretary when she's not in class at the community college."

"Why would Dante Hill's daughter need a job?" Jackson doubted she was running drugs for her father if she worked for a temp agency.

"Daddy must not have made sure his kids had enough money before we seized his accounts. I'll text you a list of the last three companies she worked for. I doubt she's still staying at the same rental property, especially if she's already had the surgery and changed her identity, but check it out anyway. Even if she's moved, maybe one of her former coworkers might have an idea where we can find her."

"And the brother?" Jackson asked.

"Martinez and Steele can hunt him down. I have a hunch he might be our shooter. He fits the physical description."

"That makes sense." Jackson felt slightly better now that they had a possible name to go with the masked face. "We also need to find the surgeon's former nurse. She quit suddenly last week. From what Bailey has told me, it sounds like she would have assisted in the surgery—that makes her a loose end." He rattled off her name and possible new location.

After concluding the call, Jackson found Bailey standing beside the dining room table, pinning her hair into a bun and then hiding it beneath Lily's tan-colored sun hat.

"You're back." Her face lit up as she pushed stray strands of hair behind her ears. "Cole and I were discussing how I should try to disguise myself before we leave the ranch. The lieutenant will be here before long."

"Good idea." Jackson turned to his brother. "We should check out the last-known address for Victoria Hill, Dante's daughter. Just to see if she left any clues behind. It's not likely that she's still living there after all the others have done to protect her."

"'We'?" Cole glanced in Bailey's direction, as a way of reminding him they had a civilian in their midst.

Jackson hadn't forgotten. He wanted to take the lead on this but couldn't if he intended to maintain his undercover status. "You'll need backup. You can't ask for help at the station without risking it getting to the leak. We'll keep a safe distance away, and Bailey's good at hiding on the floorboard," he said, tongue in cheek.

Bailey shot daggers at him with her eyes.

Cole quickly hid his amusement.

In a more serious tone, Jackson added, "Bailey, you will need to be mindful of your surroundings and duck if necessary."

Worry shadowed her brown eyes. "I'm all for helping the investigation, but won't we be walking into the lion's den if Victoria is still living there? I would feel better if we all went together in Cole's car. I assume he has a siren, which makes for a much faster and safer getaway if any of these drug traffickers start shooting."

Cole lifted a shoulder. "She makes a good point about the siren, but I don't want her near the house, even if she stays in the getaway car."

"Then it's settled," Jackson concluded. "Bailey will ride with you. When we get there, you'll be on lookout and I'll snoop around Victoria's windows. Since we don't know what she looks like now, if I see a woman inside, I'll sneak a picture."

Appearing satisfied with this new plan, Bailey turned to Cole. "If Jackson gets a picture, a plastic surgeon might be able to definitively tell you whether or not it's Victoria."

"Good to know." Cole removed his car keys from his pocket. "Let's go."

Twenty minutes later, while driving his father's truck, Jackson spotted the old ranch-style house built on a large lot, now covered with weeds and dead grass. Playing it safe, he passed it by and pulled over two blocks away. When Cole pulled up behind him, Jackson walked back to his brother's unmarked vehicle.

Cole rolled down his window. "How do you want to do this?"

"Find a spot where you can see the house from this road." Jackson sent a reassuring smile to Bailey, who sat in the passenger seat. "See you both soon."

"Call me," Cole instructed, "and keep the line between us open so I'll know if you run into any trouble."

Jackson tapped on the roof and headed back to the truck. A minute later, he pulled up in front of the rental property and called his brother. "The driveway is empty, and the shades are down. Doesn't look like anyone's home."

"Don't let your guard down," Cole warned.

With the phone tucked into his shirt pocket, Jackson exited his vehicle and walked across the dry grass toward the front door. Victoria must have been strapped for cash to rent this place.

He knew better than to stand in front of the door, where someone could shoot him from the other side. Cautiously standing to the side, he knocked and waited. No one answered.

A bird squawked and flew overhead. Other than the flapping of wings and the hum of a car engine in the far distance, he heard nothing nearby. He leaned over and peered inside through the small opening between the shade and the window frame. From what he could see, if Victoria owned furniture, it was gone now. The laminate dining room floor had been swept clean, presumably with the broom he saw propped up against the wall.

Jackson removed the phone from his shirt pocket. "The house is empty," he told Cole. About to hang up, he spotted a striped kitten meandering out of the kitchen in his direction. "She left a cat trapped inside."

"She might be coming back for it." Cole had a point, but that was still no reason to leave an animal in an empty house for who knew how long.

With a twist of the knob, Jackson pushed open the door and called for the ball of fur. "Here, kitty, kitty." The cat leaped outside. "Hey! You can't stay out here in the middle of nowhere by yourself."

Jackson chased after the little guy, who dashed toward the street. Dry Bermuda grass crunched beneath his boots as he ran. When he reached the concrete sidewalk near his father's truck, he reached his hand out for the kitten, which was hiding behind the front tire.

A roaring boom split the air behind him. Before he could react, a powerful force swept him off his feet. He landed full force onto the asphalt with the wind knocked out of his chest. Shocked and dazed, it took him a few seconds to lift his head and suck in much-needed air. He coughed and tried again.

A wave of heat and smoke floated above him as he turned to see the total destruction of the front entrance where he had been standing moments before. Orange and red infernal flames reached out to consume the rooms the bomb hadn't brought down.

"Jackson!" Cole's voice came through the cell phone he had managed to hold on to during the explosion. "Get out of there! The green muscle car is speeding this way."

TWELVE

"Do something!" Bailey yelled at Cole, who turned the keys in the ignition of his unmarked police vehicle. The ominous sound of the green muscle car's engine revving grew louder and closer by the second. The man had to be on his way to what was left of Victoria's house. Bailey's feelings for Jackson, along with her fight-or-flight instinct, demanded they act now.

She peered through the binoculars aimed at the house fully engulfed in flames. She could see Jackson struggling to stand after being blown off his feet by the explosion. "He won't escape in time without help!"

Cole's tires spewed dirt as he swung them into a sharp U-turn. They raced toward the billowing smoke. Bailey's heart pounded in her chest. They had to beat the other car to the house.

Jackson came into view, swaying on his feet.

Cole drove up over the sidewalk and slammed on his brakes. "Bailey, you're driving the truck. Find a place for you two to hide until I call you."

By the time Cole snatched Jackson's cowboy hat off the ground and guided him up into the passenger seat, Bailey had slipped behind the steering wheel and secured her seat belt. She caught the keys the detective tossed her way, and he slammed the door shut.

"I can drive," Jackson insisted, pressing fingers against his temple.

"No, you can't. Buckle up." She spotted the green muscle car a block away and floored the gas pedal. "Hold on!"

They couldn't go back the way they'd come, so she pressed forward, down a road where homes were few and far between. With one more check in the rearview mirror, she spotted a red and blue police light shining through Cole's windshield. He drew his gun over the hood, using the car for protection when the enemy turned the corner and headed straight toward him.

"Go back!" Jackson demanded, his gaze boring into the side mirror.

"We can't." Her breath hitched. She wanted to help Cole, but Jackson was in no shape to fight; and even if he had an extra gun to lend her, she couldn't shoot the side of a barn from ten feet away. They would just get in Cole's way.

"Turn around!" Jackson grabbed the wheel.

While struggling over control of the truck, they narrowly missed striking a stop sign. Jackson seemed to realize this wasn't a fight he could safely win, because he released his grip and huffed a breath.

She steered them off the curb and back onto the asphalt. "You're going to get us killed!" Sirens sliced through the tension between them. "The cavalry's on the way, and I haven't heard a single gunshot. Cole can take care of himself, and I told him that I would take care of you. Don't you dare try to stop me from keeping my word."

The multiple sirens she could now hear would have warned off even the most stubborn assailant. One cruiser sounded close enough to have reached the house.

"I won't interfere again." Settling back into his seat, Jackson added, "Unless I have to."

"I wouldn't expect anything less." Bailey focused on settling her nerves as she took the next corner in search of a safe haven. Fifteen minutes later, with Jackson staring out the window, they entered a grocery store parking lot and came to a stop in the shade of a tree at the far end. With her pulse still racing, she shut down the engine.

When he looked her way, his eyes were sharper, more focused.

She offered a weak smile. "How do you feel? That was quite an explosion back there."

"I've seen worse…on TV." He ran his hand through his disheveled hair, his hat still on the seat beside him. New scratches threatened to add another scar to his ruggedly handsome face. She never did ask him about the jagged mark on his cheek. He had been so closed off to discussing his personal life she never broached the topic.

Bailey handed him a water bottle from the cup holder. "Here, drink this. You don't want to get dehydrated."

His expression turned to one of amusement at her use of his repeated advice to her. After downing most of the bottle's contents, he wet a napkin from the glove compartment and began cleaning his face and arms. A deepening scowl relayed his discomfort each time he swiped at a fresh wound.

She cringed while watching. When he finished, she

reached out to touch the dirt he'd missed on his neck. "Here."

His gaze softened and locked on hers.

Her breath caught in her throat. Despite all her attempts to keep her distance emotionally, she'd come to realize that he had invaded her heart. Was it possible for them to have a future together? Back at the ranch, he said he wanted to talk after this was all over. Did that mean he was finally ready to tell her his secrets? If he was—and his answer was something she could live with—an open, honest relationship could lead to a deeper connection. Maybe.

He wiped his neck, not moving his gaze away from hers. "Did I get it all?"

She nodded. "You never told me—are you okay? You went down hard. Watching… I was so afraid you… died."

Jackson ran his thumb along her jaw. "I'm fine. Nothing an over-the-counter pain reliever can't fix." His cell phone rang, stealing his attention away from her. "Cole, what happened back there? Wait a second. I'll put you on speaker. Go on."

"When the guy in the green car realized I was a cop with a gun pointed at him, he fled. I gave chase, and with the help of two patrol officers, we blocked him in and made the arrest. He lawyered up the second I cuffed him."

"One bad guy down and a whole lot more to go." Bailey recognized the strain in her voice.

Jackson's frown acknowledged the truth in her statement. "Is it safe to head back to the ranch?"

"Not yet," Cole said apologetically. "Lily just called. The lieutenant is still there, trying to convince Mom and Dad they should call him immediately if they hear from you."

"And Mom hasn't thrown the lieutenant out of the house yet?"

Cole chuckled. "She's showing great restraint for your benefit. I'm heading to the station. I'll call Bailey's dad again when I get there."

"Make sure you play the recording we made," Bailey chimed in. Her father needed to clear Jackson's name.

"I won't forget," Cole assured her. "What are your plans?"

"Since we have time on our hands, we'll check out the manufacturing company where Victoria Hill temped," Jackson explained. "Someone she worked with might know where she's gone."

"If I can get away from the station, I'll join you. If not, I can follow up on any leads you dig up later." Cole disconnected the call.

"My guess is Victoria turned to smuggling drugs like her father and used the temp job to explain her income." Bailey's disapproving tone showcased her opinion on the matter.

"Or," Jackson began, the gleam of an idea in his eyes, "maybe she helped the ring smuggle drugs inside the same containers and trucks coming to or leaving the company where she worked. Let's go find someone who will talk to us. I'll drive."

Her protest slipped away in a new burst of insight when she noticed a jewelry store across the street. She suddenly remembered that Stephanie had a best friend who designed earrings and necklaces. Bailey had actually met her once, when she was in town visiting Stephanie over the holidays. Plus, Stephanie talked about her all the time, to the point where Bailey had no trouble remembering the woman's name and the name of her business. After rushing to change seats with Jackson, Bailey buckled up and shared her revelation. "If anyone can get Stephanie to call us, it's her friend in South Carolina. I'll reach out to her."

"Give it a try." Jackson handed her his phone and turned the key in the ignition.

While he drove, she searched for the woman's website and left a message at the number provided. "This is Bailey Scott. We met last December at Stephanie Carson's Christmas party. Stephanie and I worked together before she moved. It's crucial I speak to her. Lives are at stake. Please tell her this phone is safe to call."

After rattling off their contact information, Bailey ended the call and turned to Jackson. "I hope we hear back from Stephanie. And I hope she knows something helpful."

"I'm convinced whatever she saw or heard scared her enough to convince her husband they needed to leave town, cutting off all contact." Jackson turned into the industrial complex that contained the manufacturing company. "Follow my lead."

Bailey tucked stray hairs into the sun hat she wore before sliding out of the truck. Standing beside the driver's-side door, Jackson swatted away the dirt clinging to his clothing, then tipped his hat down over the scratches on his forehead.

They entered the spacious lobby, where their footsteps echoed off stark walls as they approached the young redheaded man sitting behind an information desk. He tore his attention away from the computer screen and greeted them. "Welcome to Furry Friend Foods. How can I help you today?"

"Has Detective Walker arrived yet?" Jackson glanced about as if looking for his brother.

Since they both knew that Cole was busy at the station, Bailey suspected mentioning the detective was Jackson's way of eliciting assistance without flashing a badge.

The expression on the young man's freckled face grew serious. "Uh, no. Is there a problem?"

Jackson peered down at him. "We understand a college student named Victoria Hill worked for your company as a temporary employee."

"Are you with the police?"

"We are," Jackson said matter-of-factly. He handed him one of Cole's business cards.

The redhead's eyes widened. "Yeah… Uh, I know Victoria. She left a few months ago." He leaned closer. "Is she okay? I called when she no-showed one day, but I couldn't reach her. And she never came back."

"We haven't been able to locate her." Jackson's voice took on an ominous tone. "That's why we're here. What department did she work in?"

"Payroll. I heard she worked hard, and everyone liked her. John, the guy she was dating, is a good friend of mine. They were assigned cubicles across from each other."

Bailey arched a brow. "'*Was* dating'?"

"Hey, if anything happened to her, he did not do it." Crossing his arms over his chest, the young man added, "He's not the type. They didn't even date long enough for him to turn all stalker on her. She dropped him when she left the company, and he started dating the girl who took her place."

"What's John's last name?" Jackson asked, taking back the conversation.

"Miller. He's not here right now. He took an early lunch break to sort out an issue at the bank."

Jackson eyed him speculatively, and the young man must have felt compelled to explain.

"John was about to close on a house when the bank called and said his new loan in France skewed his debt-to-income ratio, so he no longer qualified for the loan. It had to be a mistake. He's never even been to France. He's never left the country."

Could Victoria be connected to John's newfound money problems? Bailey glanced in Jackson's direction, and his expression suggested he shared her suspicion.

"One more question." Jackson tapped the glass desktop. "Is there anyone else in the company who spent a lot of time with Victoria?"

"No." He shook his head. "She was kind of quiet. Kept to herself."

"Thank you for your help," Jackson said, concluding the conversation.

Bailey assumed Cole would follow up with John Miller. There probably wasn't much more they could do here without someone asking to see a badge.

She was about to turn to leave when a nagging feeling held her back. "Has anyone else here suddenly found themselves having financial problems they couldn't explain?"

Realization lit up the boy's face. "Come to think of it, I was turned down for a department store credit card last week, which didn't make any sense. I have a good credit score."

"Hmm." Jackson appeared intrigued. "Did you find out why you were rejected?"

"I was too embarrassed to ask. I applied at the check-out counter, and there was a long line of people behind me."

Bailey offered a sympathetic smile and glanced at his name tag. "Again, thank you for your help, Howard."

After returning to the truck, Jackson shoved his key into the ignition. "Great question back there." His eyes shone with admiration when he turned his gaze on her. "I wonder how many people Victoria used her position in Payroll to steal from so she could funnel money to her father."

"I'd guess quite a few," Bailey said, buckling her seat belt, "and someone found out. That would explain why Victoria needed to change her looks."

The young man they'd spoken to had left his desk and now stood at the glass door. Next to him was a middle-aged woman wearing a long-sleeved burgundy shirt and gray pencil skirt. He pointed in their direction.

"We've attracted unwanted attention—we should get out of here." Jackson shifted into Reverse as the woman marched outside toward them.

Jackson headed back to the ranch after Cole sent them an all-clear text. This time, Bailey had a front-seat view of his family's expansive property as they entered the back gate and drove over the unpaved road. He parked next to the white post-and-rail fencing to show her the chestnut-colored quarter horses frolicking in the sunny meadow.

A sense of peace settled over him. In that quiet moment, he whispered a thankful prayer. He was convinced God had used the kitten to lure him away from the explosion.

Bailey rolled down her window and leaned out of the pickup truck for a better look. "They're beautiful!" She turned back to him, eyes filled with wonder. "I would love to ride again one day soon. I'm a bit rusty, but I'm sure you have a trail horse who wouldn't send me flying into a bush."

Her gaze lingered on him long enough to warm his heart and make him crave more moments like this one.

His phone chimed before he could tell her he wanted nothing more than to explore his childhood home on horseback with her. He glanced at the screen. "I don't recognize the number."

"It could be Stephanie. Put it on speaker." Bailey scooted closer.

About to answer, he held the phone between them. "You do the talking."

"Hello?" Bailey said.

"Bailey? Is that you?" a woman's voice replied.

"Yes. Hi, Stephanie. Thank you so much for calling me."

"I heard lives were at stake." The nurse's voice wobbled with apprehension. "What's going on?"

Bailey's anguished expression tore at Jackson's heart.

"Dr. Daniels and Amy are both dead. They were murdered by a masked shooter, who is now chasing me. I can't go home. I have to hide from him and his associates." Bailey gripped her pendant tightly. "I know about Victoria Hill's secret surgery. These men were sent by her father, who's deeply involved in drug smuggling. Is that why you quit so suddenly?"

Silence filled the truck's cabin. Finally, the nurse answered, "I am so sorry." Stephanie's breath hitched as she spoke. "Daniels promised to protect everyone."

Bailey gaped. "I don't understand. The doctor knew this might happen? How?"

Stephanie sniffled. "Remember Tanya? The dental assistant who took smoke breaks in the parking lot?"

"Yeah…" Bailey met Jackson's gaze. All roads led back to Dr. York's dental office.

"Tanya told me the woman we operated on was a Mafia-type princess and that the men in her father's organization were getting their teeth altered by the dentist. Tanya overheard the dentist telling his wife that her cousin and his buddies planned to fake their deaths. He could tell by the work they wanted done."

"We—Jackson, the handyman from the medical complex, and I—know that much."

"Then you must have also figured out that once these people get what they want—we are all loose ends that need to be tied off. It's in their best interests to kill us. Dead people can't testify in court."

The color drained from Bailey's face, and Jackson gave her shoulder a reassuring touch, but she only stared at the phone as Stephanie continued to speak.

"That's why I left. Tanya told me these guys scared her to death when she helped work on them. They were armed during their procedures. She was applying for jobs in Phoenix under her maiden name and said we were in danger, too, since we know what this celebrity looks like now."

"I don't." Conviction steeled Bailey's tone.

"Yeah, but there are before-and-after pictures. As far as these thugs know, you could have seen them—or her. They can't take that chance."

Stephanie's words confirmed what Jackson had suspected. Pictures of Victoria's new face existed, and the shooter sent the kid to the doctor's house to find them.

"So how was Dr. Daniels supposed to protect us?" Bailey stiffened her body and her resolve. "And where are these pictures now?"

"Daniels hid the pictures. He planned to use them as leverage if they ever threatened us."

"Well, they bypassed *threatening* and chose homicide." Anger hardened Bailey's words.

"I was afraid of that. It's why I convinced my husband we should move out of state."

"And you didn't think to tell us that we weren't safe, either? Amy is dead, and I'm running for my life."

Stephanie's sobs choked her words. "I… I'm so sorry. Daniels swore he'd tell the both of you."

"He didn't." Bailey slowly shook her head, betrayal evident in her expression. "Do you know where he hid the pictures?"

"His RV. It's parked on Bear's empty lot behind his store. There's a spare key in the cash register."

Jackson mouthed, "Bear?"

Bailey lifted a finger, indicating he should wait for her to explain. "And where exactly are these pictures?"

"Daniels didn't say. I truly am sorry. Please forgive me. I hate that you're going through this."

"I know you have a kind heart." Bailey's expression and voice softened. "Stephanie, did you really move to Hawaii?"

"No."

"Don't tell me where you are. Just in case… And stay safe. I'll pass a message back to your friend when it's over so she can let you know." After she ended the call, Bailey leaned back against the seat, and a deep sadness fell over her face. "Dr. Daniels should have told us."

"You're right. I don't know what he was thinking," Jackson said. "Maybe he didn't want to worry you, but you had the right to know. He should have allowed you to choose between staying or leaving."

"At least we know where to find the pictures." Her tone held a hint of hope. "Cole can use them to locate Victoria. Maybe she'll tell him who the shooter is and where he's hiding."

"Are you going to tell me where this empty lot is, or are you going to make me take you with me?"

A smile tugged at her lips. "You already know the answer."

"I do." This time, he'd have Cole follow them in case they ran into trouble again. Jackson pushed open the door to the truck. "I need to stretch my legs and make a couple of calls before we leave." It would only take a few minutes to tell Cole and his DEA supervisor what they had learned. It felt good to have real news to share for once.

If they found these pictures before the drug ring, the good guys would finally have the upper hand. The race was on.

THIRTEEN

Bailey kept an eye out for the shooter while Jackson drove them down the state road, leaving the red rocks of Sedona behind them. "You'll want to slow down," she warned. "The turnoff to Bear's store is a green street sign partially hidden by a paloverde tree. It's hard to see until you're on top of it."

Jackson handed her his phone before easing on the brakes in preparation for the turn. "Text Cole the directions. He's a few minutes behind us."

She gladly complied, impatient to talk with the detective and learn more about his call to her father. Jackson continued to check his rearview mirror for anyone tailing them. Another car in the vicinity would stick out on this paved two-lane road cutting through rugged terrain.

"That's Bear's place." She pointed to the General Store, a small white building on the side of the road.

Jackson pulled into one of the parking lot's four marked spaces, all of which were empty. "How do you know this guy?"

"He went to medical school with Dr. Daniels."

Jackson raised his brow in surprise.

His reaction, although expected, still tickled her. "His father and grandfather were both doctors. When Bear decided medical school wasn't for him, he quit and opened this place. By then, he'd formed a lifelong friendship with Daniels." *Lifelong* repeated in her mind, and her chest tightened. Daniels's life hadn't been long enough. She was upset that he'd kept secrets from her; but despite all that, she knew he'd been a good person at heart, just like his friend was. "Bear's a great guy. You'll see." She managed to push aside her grief. For now.

They slipped out of the truck and into the store. A short, thin man wearing faded jeans and a cartoon T-shirt turned from stocking candy shelves when the bell above the door chimed. He beamed when he spotted them.

"Bailey!" He hurried over and gathered her in a fierce embrace.

Realization registered on Jackson's handsome face. "Bear."

She chuckled. "As in *bear hugs*."

The owner of the establishment stood back to rake his gaze over her. "You look great for someone who's been shot at and kidnapped."

"Not kidnapped," Bailey corrected. "But still trying to evade shooters." After making the introductions, she felt a grim smile fall into place. "I am so sorry about Dr. Daniels. I know how close you were."

He took her hands in his and squeezed. "We both admired and respected him. God bless his soul."

"I pray for him every day." *And always will.* "Bear, we are trying to help Jackson's brother, who's the Sedona detective working the murder case. I spoke to

Stephanie, and she said Daniels had evidence in his RV. I need to go out there and find it."

Bear ran a hand through his graying hair. "I guess that would be okay. My name is still on the title to the RV since he hadn't finished making the payments. I was willing to give it to his sister, but she's devastated and told me that she can't emotionally deal with it or whatever he stored inside—unless he was hiding wads of cash or piles of gold." A weak chortle escaped his lips. "Her sense of humor, even in times of trouble, reminds me of her brother. He always made me laugh."

Bailey had witnessed that side of the doctor whenever he tore his mind away from work or from the problems in this personal life. Tears pricked her eyes as happy memories mingled with a keen sense of loss.

Jackson interrupted the moment. "Did Daniels ever mention performing a secret surgery on a celebrity?"

"Never—but that's not surprising, with privacy laws the way they are."

"The doc would have kept his lips tight anyway," she added. The man had integrity. But he also showed his emotions in his expressions, making him easy to read if you stopped to pay attention. "Bear, did you ever get the impression Daniels was afraid of something or someone?"

He leaned back against the cash register counter near a display of chewing gum and mints. "Doc did say to call him if anyone poked around his RV. I thought he was worried teenagers might break in or vandalize it." A frown marred his features. "Do you think he knew the guy who shot him?"

Bailey shrugged. "It's possible."

"*Has* anyone been snooping around?" Jackson

asked. Before Bear could answer, the sound of a vehicle crunching gravel jerked Jackson's attention to the parking lot behind him, where his brother was pulling in.

"I haven't seen any trespassers, and I live out back." Bear opened the cash register drawer, lifted the tray and retrieved a key. "Doc's RV has teal-and-purple stripes. The other one is mine."

"Thanks, Bear." Bailey accepted the key with a grateful heart. "We'll bring it back before we leave."

She followed Jackson out the door and over to Cole, who was exiting his unmarked vehicle. He wore his all-business demeanor like a coat. That didn't stop her from asking, "Now, will you please tell me what my father said?"

"Sorry to make you wait." Cole pushed his door shut. "The police station's walls have ears."

Bailey slumped, feeling petty for her burst of indignation. "You're right. I let myself forget for a few minutes. I'm sorry—I know you're dealing with a lot."

"It's fine. Your father got back to me after I left a message with the recording you made. He confessed he had been avoiding me because the reporter lied about his last call to the police station, and he didn't know who to trust." Cole's gaze shifted to his brother. "After I heard what he had to say, I transferred the call to the lieutenant's office and placed it on speaker."

Jackson spoke through a clenched jaw. "Am I still a person of interest?"

"No." Cole shook his head, and a wave of relief eased the tension in the air. "Her father made it emphatically clear that Bailey told him you were protecting her and she went with you willingly."

"What about the reporter?" Bailey rubbed her pendant, hoping she was finally a step closer to going home to her father. "Will the lieutenant do something about her?"

"He's holding a press conference today where he'll clear Jackson's name. The reporter will look bad—and to make the department look good, he'll announce they've made an arrest in connection with the shooting."

"Two," Bailey corrected. "There are two men in custody. The one from Dr. Daniels's garage and the man driving the green muscle car."

Cole's gaze darted to his brother, and she wondered what that was all about.

"They might choose to keep some information quiet when it comes to who they have in custody, especially when that information includes a potential informant." Jackson took several steps away from them. "Bear gave us permission to search the RV. Let's go."

"I'll take the lead." Cole crossed the asphalt to the corner of the store and entered the empty dirt lot. All three surveyed the area around them every step of the way. Two recreational vehicles and a metal shed formed an L-shape at the far edge of the leveled acre of land.

"The RV with stripes," Bailey announced. They passed the other, more expensive home away from home, with fancy scrollwork on the sides and slide-outs to expand the inner living space. "Now I can see why Bear sold his old RV to the doctor. This one is much nicer."

Jackson gave it a critical once-over. "I wouldn't mind camping in a rig like this."

"Only if you take me with you," Cole added.

Bailey had never been camping but could imagine the possibility. If her life ever returned to a new normal.

"You should wait here," Cole suggested when they

neared the older second vehicle. "Use the shed for cover if needed."

She could see it wouldn't do her any good to argue, so she dropped the key into his palm and then watched the detective disappear inside. The slight possibility someone might be lying in wait agitated her nerves. "We should be able to go in with him. Bear said no one has been here."

"Cole needs to do his job," Jackson said, his tone calm and understanding. "It'll only take a minute."

"You're right." She breathed easier, though, when Cole poked his head out the open door to give them the all clear.

Jackson held her hand as she ascended the metal steps one at a time, and she appreciated the reassuring warmth of his touch.

Inside, she found herself stepping first into a clean and tidy kitchenette. Cole was already opening and closing cabinets. Jackson squeezed past him to investigate the sleeping quarters.

Bailey took her time combing through the storage compartments near the sofa. Nothing of interest. Mainly books on fishing, thriller novels, some eyeglass cleaner and a throw blanket. She turned, and her gaze landed on the cramped eating space with drawers tucked under the bench seats.

Once Cole moved out of her way, she crouched beneath the table and tugged open a drawer to rummage through crossword puzzle books and a paint-by-numbers set. In the farthest corner of the drawer, she found a cardboard box decorated with a floral design. She reached in and pulled out the facial tissue in one big clump, and a hidden thumb drive fell to the vinyl floor. Excitement shot through her.

"I found it!" She bumped into the table in her rush to jump up and hold the thumb drive high. "At least, I think so."

"Let's see." Jackson headed in her direction.

"We can plug it into your old laptop back at the ranch," Cole told his brother while digging an evidence bag out of his pocket. "I don't dare take this to the police station."

"Even I know the leak would make it vanish." Bailey dropped the thumb drive into the bag, feeling triumphant for finding a key piece of evidence. She hoped the device held the post–cosmetic surgery pictures. Then the police could hunt down and interrogate Victoria.

"Speaking of leaks," Jackson said, capturing their attention, "I have a plan to trap this one."

Back at the ranch, Jackson entered the kitchen and found his eldest brother, Zach, wolfing down chocolate chip cookies. He stood a few inches taller than the other Walkers, and his dark hair resembled their father's at a much younger age.

"I hope you saved some for us," Jackson teased, glad to see another sibling home to help protect the family.

"Look what the cat dragged in," Zach shot back, a huge grin lighting up his face.

"I didn't think you were making it back until late tonight."

"I arranged for an earlier flight after Dad called." He hugged Jackson and then leaned to the side. "This must be the sweet and pretty Bailey I keep hearing about."

"Look in your little black book if you need a date,"

Jackson said protectively. Zach was a charmer who had taken many women out for a first date but rarely a second. "Bailey is busy running from drug traffickers."

Zach chuckled and turned to their mother, who set the timer for another batch of cookies. "You were right, Mom. He likes her."

Jackson wasn't surprised she'd shared her insights with Zach. She wanted all her sons to start families of their own as soon as possible and start giving her grandbabies. Avoiding that discussion, he took Bailey's hand and directed her toward the dining room. "We have work to do. I'll catch up with you later."

Cole snatched a cookie from the kitchen island with an amused grin spread across his face. "Welcome home."

"Thanks." Zach turned and called out, "I don't have a little black book."

"Nice to meet you," Bailey tossed back over her shoulder.

Jackson sat in front of the laptop he'd left on the table. Bailey and Cole pulled chairs to either side of him as he booted up the computer and inserted the thumb drive. He was surprised to find a single file labeled *Marissa Myers*.

Bailey's eyes widened. "I recognize that name from my paperwork. She paid in cash for several procedures."

Jackson moved the cursor over the first picture and clicked. Victoria Hill popped up on the screen. "Meet Marissa."

"If that's the name she gave to Daniels and the hospital," Cole said, studying the screen, "I highly doubt she's going by it now. That would be foolish."

"True." Jackson clicked on a picture dated a month

after the first one. "Brace yourself. We're about to meet the new Marissa, aka Victoria."

The woman staring back at them appeared to be a different person, except for her large green eyes. Thanks to a stylist, Victoria's once long, dark hair was now short and auburn. Daniels had narrowed her nose, plumped up her cheeks and filled her lips. She was more attractive than before but not stunning—not so eye-catching that she'd draw too much attention.

Jackson sat back to give the others a better view.

"Nice work," Cole said. "I wouldn't know it was Victoria."

"Looking at the picture, I'm positive I never saw her after the surgery." Grief permeated Bailey's tone. "She's the reason Dr. Daniels and Amy are dead. This makes me sick to my stomach. Couldn't they have found a corrupt surgeon willing to do their dirty work? One they wouldn't need to kill?"

"Apparently not." Jackson reached down and held her hand, hoping to convey his understanding and concern. "We'll catch these guys. And Victoria."

"I believe you." Bailey's brown eyes darkened, and he wanted nothing more than to lean close and press his lips to hers, but he couldn't. Not here. Not now.

His phone dinged, alerting him to a text message from Mike, who said he had news. "I need to make a call." He scooted the chair back. "Look through the other pictures while I'm gone."

Withdrawing to his childhood bedroom, Jackson pressed the phone number on his cell phone and waited impatiently.

"We heard from Interpol," Mike stated, cutting straight to business. "Victoria Hill stole the personal information of a whole slew of employees at her temp jobs, as you suspected. Her father used their clean credit histories to secure loans and purchase property he's been using to hide out. French police raided one of the houses and barely missed catching Dante. It was obvious he knew they were coming."

"That explains the need for Victoria's cosmetic surgery." Discussing the drug kingpin and his daughter brought on the urge to peer out through his bedroom window. He refused to let his guard down even though all he could see was a typical tranquil day on the ranch. If nothing else, this case had taught him how danger could lurk behind any innocent corner. "We have the before-and-after photos Daniels took. I'll send them to you, along with the name she used."

Upon returning to the dining room, he found Lily and Zach inspecting the laptop screen. "If you ever see that woman," Jackson told them, "get away and call…" His glance fell on Bailey. "Cole. Call Cole immediately. The men who protect Victoria will shoot anyone who might recognize her."

Zach cringed. "I won't be adding *her* number to my nonexistent little black book."

Lily rolled her eyes.

Jackson kept his focus glued to the computer screen while reclaiming his seat next to Bailey. "That was a friend of mine on the phone. Interpol is on to Victoria. That's why she had to change her looks."

"And kill anyone who could prove this Marissa is Victoria." A deep sadness fell over Bailey's expression.

Lily placed both hands on Bailey's shoulders, offering the comfort Jackson wanted to provide. Shifting his mind back to business, he announced, "I have a plan to uncover the identity of the leak at the police station."

Cole straightened in his seat. "I've been waiting to hear this."

"Good," Jackson began, "because you have the starring role. Tell the lieutenant—and anyone else at the station you can think of—that I found Dr. Daniels's before-and-after pictures of Victoria Hill, who is now a redhead. Let them know that I was on my way back from Phoenix when I called and will hand over the thumb drive when I reach Sedona."

"Mentioning her hair color will give the story legitimacy," Cole pointed out. "I can see why we need to pretend you found the pictures. If we say I did, I would be forced to give up the thumb drive."

Zach whistled. "You're going to light a fire under the drug princess and her henchmen. We'd better sleep with guns close by."

Cole jerked a thumb in their older brother's direction. "I filled him in on everything."

Jackson nodded. "We all need to know what we're dealing with here."

Bailey's face paled. "I should stay somewhere else. I don't want to put any of you in danger. You've all been so kind to me."

"Don't be ridiculous," their mother said from the corner of the dining room, drying her hands with a dish towel. "We care about you, Bailey, and we will do what it takes to protect you."

"Thank you." Tears welled up in her eyes.

Jackson couldn't resist any longer. He reached his arm around her. Lily stepped back, making room for him. "Bailey, everything's going to be okay. I prayed over it, and I feel it in my soul."

She leaned closer. "I..." Choking on her words, she stopped trying to speak and buried her face in his chest.

He held her close while avoiding eye contact with anyone else in the room. There was no need to look to know their reactions. Most would be shocked. Others delighted.

As if suddenly aware of their audience, Bailey sat up.

Jackson reluctantly pulled his arm back.

"I'm going to make those calls." Cole pushed out of his chair and left the room.

Lily claimed his seat. "What can I do?"

"Keep an eye on our property with the drone," Jackson instructed. "You handle that thing better than anyone else."

"I do," she said with pride.

"And me?" Zach asked.

"Make sure the guns and ammo are ready to use. These drug traffickers know who I am, thanks to that reporter. They probably already know about the ranch."

"We can handle anything they throw at us," Zach assured him.

"You can say that again." Their mother sent Jackson a warm smile. "Update your father when he comes back from the feedstore."

Jackson nodded, hoping they were right about being able to handle things here.

Over the next hour, Bailey helped his mother prepare dinner while Jackson went outside and inspected images sent from the drone. Nothing appeared out of place. "Good job, Lily. Send her back up every fifteen minutes."

"Will do." Lily carried the drone into the garage.

Cole stepped outside through the kitchen door and grinned. "Your plan worked. The leak was caught in the act, demanding the return of blackmail photos that were used against them in exchange for information on where they could find Victoria's before-and-after photographs."

"Who was it?" Jackson feared it might be someone they called a friend.

"Nicole, the lieutenant's secretary. I would have never dreamed it possible, but she was caught on the phone with the dentist's wife."

"The lieutenant's secretary." Jackson mulled over this new development. The woman would have been privy to most information dealing with the drug traffickers, either through phone messages or overhearing discussions through the thin office wall behind her desk. "It makes sense. Bailey's father did leave a message for the lieutenant with her."

"Which Nicole claimed had already been given to a dispatcher. That much was true," Cole admitted. "At least, partially. The dispatcher heard part of what the father had to say before she redirected the call."

"What blackmail did they have on Nicole?" Jackson had met the young woman several times, and she never seemed the type to get into trouble.

"She confessed to trying cocaine with a friend, who took pictures."

"Was this friend associated with drug traffickers?"

"Dating one of them," Cole revealed. "The boyfriend used the pictures to blackmail Nicole into providing any police information they wanted—or making certain pieces of information disappear. He gave her the dentist's wife's cell number to call. She'll be arrested, too, once she returns from her family trip."

"*If* she comes back," Jackson clarified. "In the meantime, she'll pass on the message we planted."

"Which will scare the traffickers into action."

"Whatever that might be." Jackson knew he had ignited a bomb, and they all needed to prepare for the fallout.

FOURTEEN

Later that evening, with most of the family outside attending to chores, Bailey sat on the living room sofa, listening to Cole describe the plan his superiors had approved. He had used the leak's cell phone to text the dentist's wife, offering a trade. When the members of the drug ring showed up for the exchange, they'd be walking into a trap.

Jackson peered outside through the sliding glass door and then turned to his brother. "You think they'll fall for it?"

"I do," Cole said matter-of-factly. "It's what they're expecting to happen. Nicole's done a good job up to now of getting them whatever they ask for. They won't be surprised that she's pulled it off again. Since members of the ring plan to fake their deaths and leave town, they won't need those blackmail pictures much longer anyway."

Won't need. The words echoed in Bailey's mind. "They'll kill her. She's a witness, and we all know they kill witnesses."

Cole sat in the chair across from the sofa, his expression sympathetic. "They'll try, but she won't be

there. They're the ones walking into a trap, not her.
The point is to arrest whoever shows up and hope they
flip on the others."

Bailey wanted them to catch the entire ring in one
fell swoop. Two were already behind bars, but how
many more were left? Concerned for Jackson's brother,
she asked, "Are you going to be there?"

"It's my plan." Cole stood. "I need to leave now. We
have a lot to do before midnight." An unspoken message to be careful appeared to pass between the brothers on the detective's way out.

Jackson claimed the spot on the sofa beside her.
Since this was a police operation, he had to stay behind at the ranch. That thought gave her comfort.

He reached over and squeezed her hand. "The lieutenant sent two uniformed officers. One's in front, and
the other is in the back. With the leak out of the way,
we can trust these guys."

Fatigue weighed her down. Would this nightmare
ever end? "If the drug traffickers think they're getting what they want from Nicole, then why do we need
guards?"

"For the same reason as before. We know what Victoria looks like."

How could she have forgotten? Victoria was their
drug-ring princess. Daughter of the kingpin. By com-
parison, Bailey was an expendable peasant from the
neighboring kingdom. And Jackson? She met his gaze,
and a ripple of attraction flowed through their joined
hands to her heart. He was a noble knight willing to
risk his life for her.

She blinked away the fairy tale, afraid there was no

happy ending ahead. "Thank you for all you've done. If anything happened to you, I—"

"It won't." He lifted her chin with his finger, guiding her gaze up to meet his.

Lost in his warm blue eyes, Bailey leaned closer, unable to stop herself. He glanced down at her lips, and her heart skipped a beat. Would he? Should they?

Taking the plunge, she closed her eyes. Jackson's lips touched hers, and she instantly released any doubt she'd ever held about their growing relationship. This felt so right. As if sharing her thoughts, he pulled her closer. Leaning into his embrace, she floated away on the warmth and tenderness of their kiss.

The sound of the kitchen door opening ended their moment together. He pulled back. "We will get through this, Bailey. And then, we'll…talk."

Talk. That's right. He wanted to tell me something. But did she want to hear it?

His mother poked her head out of the kitchen. "How about some fresh lemonade?"

"That would be great, Mom." After she retreated, Jackson ran his thumb over Bailey's bottom lip, and her longing for another kiss grew warm in her chest. The one he pressed to her forehead would have to suffice for now.

Over the next couple of hours, Jackson's family gathered in the living room to watch comedy movies in an attempt to distract themselves. It didn't work. They all waited impatiently to hear back from Cole.

Her eyelids grew heavy at a quarter to midnight, and she leaned her head back against the sofa. The moment she drifted off, a sudden gunshot blast in the distance jolted her awake. "What was that?"

With the family's attention jerked away from the television, Mrs. Walker used the remote to flip off the movie.

Mr. Walker rushed to the front window and pushed aside the blinds. The uniformed officer standing on the other side of the glass told him to stay put and keep the doors locked. "I'll radio it in and check the area."

Bailey clutched her hands together and strained to hear any noise emanating from outside.

Jackson, Zach and Lily immediately grabbed weapons from the gun cabinet hanging on the wall and spread out through the house to peer out windows and scan their surroundings. Mrs. Walker scooted closer to Bailey on the sofa. "It's probably just someone from a neighboring ranch shooting at a pesky raccoon."

"Sure," Bailey answered, hoping the woman was right even as she feared the worst.

"Fire!" Mr. Walker whipped around to his family. "The barn's on fire."

Zach beat his father to the door. "Dad, stay here and keep an eye on Bailey. Jackson and I can put out the flames."

"No." Bailey shook her head rapidly, fear threatening to overwhelm her. "It's a trap. They'll shoot you both the second you step outside."

Jackson's gaze locked on hers. "We have to free the horses. We'll be okay. I promise."

That was a promise he shouldn't make—one that he couldn't possibly be sure he'd be able to keep. But God had a plan, and she just had to hope it involved keeping him alive. She couldn't lose him.

"Let's take a truck," he suggested to Zach. "It'll give us cover."

"Take my car instead." The urgency in his mother's voice made it a demand. "You can get inside without anyone seeing you."

Jackson grabbed his sister's arm while rushing toward the kitchen. "Open the garage and shoot anyone who tries to sneak inside."

"I'll call 911 and fill them in on our situation." Mr. Walker snatched a cell phone from the coffee table. Soon, his face twisted into a mask of frustration. He tried once again with another phone to no avail. "They're using a jammer. We're on our own."

The situation seemed hopeless. With a wave of despair flowing over her, Bailey listened intently to the faint sound of an automatic garage door opening, exposing both the car and its occupants to whatever dangers lay outside. The vehicle screamed as it tore out of the enclosed space. Sitting on the edge of her seat, she held her breath, waiting for what came next. Instead of immediate gunfire, she heard gears kicking into action, signaling the garage door closing.

Mr. Walker kept vigil at the front window. When she tried to join him, he waylaid her. "You need to stay down and out of sight. Those thugs are here for you. We don't want to make the job easy for them."

"I'm so sorry." Tears welled in her eyes. "This is all my fault. Your family is in danger because of me."

He shook his head. "The drug traffickers are at fault. Don't let them off the hook by trying to take the blame." His commanding sense of authority reminded her of her father.

"You're right." She found strength in his words.

Gunshots rang out, and Bailey jumped. The blasts

were closer than before. Near the barn, if she were to hazard a guess.

Mrs. Walker patted her arm reassuringly. "It'll be okay."

The car's engine grew louder as it passed by the front of the house.

"Aren't you afraid?" Bailey searched the woman's eyes.

"Terrified," she whispered, lifting her shaking hand to prove her point. "But I can't do anything to help my boys right now. I can help you."

Bailey nodded. "Should we hide somewhere?"

Lily returned from the garage and grimaced as she stepped up to a window positioned three feet away from her father. A bullet broke the glass, whizzed by her ear and lodged into the far wall. They all dropped to the floor. On her way down, Bailey bumped into the coffee table and flinched when she knocked over a bronze statue of a horse that landed on the area rug near her hand.

"Everyone all right?" Mr. Walker called out, his tone heavy with concern.

"Yes," Bailey's voice cracked on the word. "Where's the police officer?"

"I don't hear him," Mrs. Walker said from her prone position on the floor across the table from Bailey. All color had drained from her face.

Lily soldier-crawled closer to them. She displayed the same determined features her brothers did in dangerous situations. Bailey wondered if all ranchers were this tough.

The sound of glass shattering in one of the bedrooms had Bailey clenching her teeth and inching closer to the sofa. If only she could slip beneath it and hide. *God, please guide and protect us in our time of need. This family has gone out of their way to help me. They are good people and don't deserve to die.*

"Stay down." Mr. Walker pushed to his feet. "Lily, be ready." With his gun at his side, he skulked down the hall.

Lily hid behind the end of the sofa with her rifle.

Bailey debated running into the kitchen. Would the room provide more protection, or would it just trap her in a confined area?

Before she could make a decision, a large burly man shoved Mr. Walker into the living room with a gun aimed at the back of his head. "Move," he growled.

Terror rippled through every cell of her body, but she forced herself to breathe and think. She knew she had to do something. But what?

Her fingers curled around the statue.

The tattooed man with long, dirty hair scanned the room. When he spied Bailey, his features twisted into a sinister smile, and he turned the gun on her. "There you are."

Bailey froze. This was it. In what could be her last moment on Earth, all she could think about was Jackson.

Mr. Walker kicked backward with his boot, striking his captor in the shin at the same time he elbowed him in the ribs. With his next move, he grabbed for the gun, but his attempt failed.

This was her chance. Bailey jumped up onto her knees and threw the statue with every ounce of energy she could summon. The heavy bronze object connected with the goon's forehead. He let out a yelp, then pressed a hand to the wound and stumbled back a step.

A moment later, Lily sprang up from her hiding place and took aim.

Mr. Walker dove out of the way, and Lily shot the tattooed man in the chest near his shoulder. He tried to lift his gun, and she fired again. He wobbled and his eyes rolled back in his head. Then he fell forward with a resounding thud.

Jackson's heart pounded in his ears as he gripped the steering wheel tightly. With the full moon guiding the way, he careened around a tree and sped toward the open gate leading to the burning barn. In the distance, monstrous orange flames clawed at the night sky while threatening to take the lives of their horses.

Suddenly, the windshield shattered. The bullet punching through hit the rearview mirror and went flying. Jackson covered his face with his arm. "Watch out!"

Zach leaned out the passenger-side window and aimed at a shadowy figure about to unleash a second round. The explosive sound of his brother's gun firing echoed throughout the car. "I missed him!"

"He'll come back after us. Keep your eyes open." Jackson pushed back his fear as he peered through the windows, searching for movement in the dark. "I'll drop you off at the barn door. Check for anyone inside before you release the horses."

"What are you going to do?" Zach spared a glance in his direction before the car flew over a mound in the grassy field, forcing him to grab a handhold.

With his stomach in his throat, Jackson maintained control of the car as it hit the ground with a hard bounce. "I'll drive around back to put out the fire."

"You need cover."

"I can shoot and hold a hose at the same time."

"I'm sure you can." Zach turned in his seat and checked behind them. "I'll grab the fire extinguishers as soon as the horses are free and join you."

He wouldn't be able to stop his brother from helping even if he tried. Their father's words repeated in Jackson's mind: *Every member of the Walker family can take care of themselves.* "Make it fast."

The sounds of horse screams and pounding of hooves against stall walls warred with the crackling of flames as Jackson closed the distance to the barn. With the car providing protection, Zach pushed open the passenger door and rushed over to the barn door, shoving aside the wood panel. An escaped quarter horse galloped past Zach, almost knocking him out of the way, and jumped right over the trunk of the car.

"Whoa." Jackson watched in awe until his gaze caught on a man in all black, leaning away from a tree trunk to lift a weapon in his direction. Jackson whipped his gun out of its holster, but before he could fire off a shot, the assailant doubled over and fell to the ground.

Surprised, Jackson's gaze swept the area in search of the shooter. Special Agent Martinez rose from behind a bush, the glow from the fire illuminating his rough features. Jackson offered a nod of appreciation and released the car's brakes. He drove around back, ready to put the hoses to work. Martinez jogged behind the vehicle, sticking close to trees and bushes whenever possible.

Jackson parked, jumped out of the car and ran toward the water spigot. "Cover me!" he yelled, then coughed to clear the smoke slithering down his throat. Once the water streamed from the nozzle at full force, he pulled the hose toward the raging blaze.

The horses thundered away from the barn and ran toward the far end of the ranch. While Martinez hid between the car and a clump of bushes, sirens in the distance gave Jackson hope. *Lord, please send them our way.*

Another shot rang out. Jackson whipped around and caught a glimpse of another gunman falling away. His eyes widened. *And thank you, Lord, for the agent keeping me alive.*

Zach rounded the corner carrying an industrial-size fire extinguisher in the crook of each arm. Without saying a word, he set one down and pulled the pin on the other. He used a wide sweeping motion to tackle the flames ten feet away from where Jackson worked.

The shrill sound of approaching emergency vehicles grew louder. A hook-and-ladder truck followed half a dozen squad cars. Jackson continued to fight the blaze. The police officers would have to secure the scene before the firefighters could come closer.

Several long minutes later, with the contents of both extinguishers emptied and Zach working with the third one he'd found in the trunk of their mother's car, Cole swooped in and relieved Jackson of the hose. "I ran into Agent Steele. He took out a guy who shot into the house, and Lily handled the man who held Dad captive."

Jackson's heart skipped a beat. "What?"

"Bailey's fine." Cole aimed at the diminishing flames. "Everyone inside is safe and sound. I made sure before I ran over here."

The shouts of officers on the property announced progress in capturing the attackers. The fire truck's siren sliced through the night as it continued its trek to the barn.

With firefighters about to take over the battle to control the fire, all he could think about was Bailey. He had to see with his own eyes that she was okay. Without another moment's delay, he ran toward the house.

Floodlights positioned at the corners of their home lit his path to the front door. Inside, he found the lieutenant requesting medical assistance on his cell phone, near an unconscious man. Jackson stared a moment longer than he intended, hating the fact he hadn't been here for Bailey. The lieutenant glanced up at him and pointed beyond the dining table, not missing a beat in his conversation.

The second he spotted Bailey sitting in the kitchen nook with his parents and sister, a surge of relief overwhelmed him. The fear he'd held tight in his chest melted away when she ran into his arms. Jackson held her close and thanked God for looking after the woman he was falling in love with. He avoided the looks on the faces of his family members, not allowing anything to intrude on this moment.

"I was so worried about you," Bailey whispered before burying her head in his chest.

The words Jackson wanted to express got stuck in his throat. He wanted to be alone and free of secrets before he admitted he was falling in love with her. Instead, he kept her close—her warmth passing through his shirt, straight to his heart.

Finally, he released her from his embrace and took a step back. His hands slid down her arms to take hold of her hands. "What happened in the living room?" he asked, noticing the way his mother tightly gripped her mug, no doubt filled with chamomile tea.

"Bailey saved my life." His father's answer came

with a reassuring smile. When Lily coughed, he added, "The thug got the slip on me, but your girlfriend there distracted him by throwing a statue at his face, allowing your sister to put a bullet in his chest."

Girlfriend. Maybe one day soon, she would be. He hated to leave, but now that he knew she was safe, he needed updates on the situation outside. "Good job." He squeezed Bailey's hands and sent a warm smile to Lily. "Dad, you were right. Everyone here can take care of themselves."

His father nodded. "But we always do better as a team. A family."

"True." Since Jackson had started praying again, he repeatedly asked for clarity and direction. With everything unfolding the way it had over the past few hours, he knew God had watched over them. A peace he'd never known before settled in his heart. He took comfort in knowing this feeling would empower him to deal with whatever came his way. "I'll be back soon."

Outside, he found Cole overseeing the loading of assailants into the backs of squad cars. Flashlights swept the grounds as other law enforcement personnel searched for anyone lurking in the dark. Firefighters continued working on the barn, and an EMT carried a gurney to the location where one of the shooters had gone down.

Jackson waited for his brother to reach him before asking, "What happened with the trade you set up earlier? It looks like these guys timed their attack here to coincide with your meeting."

"They must have suspected a trap." Cole frowned while rubbing the back of his neck. "Only one guy showed up for the exchange. He surrendered the second he realized he was surrounded, but he isn't telling us anything other than his name."

Jackson huffed a breath. "Well, I'm glad all of you came here when you did. Who knows what might have happened otherwise?"

"You can thank the officer who was guarding the back of the house. He tried to report a gunshot, but someone used a jammer to block communication with the ranch. He had to walk out of the device's range to reach us."

"Then what happened to him?"

"He tripped on a gopher hole and broke his leg. There was no way he could make it back to help fight these guys. The other officer was knocked out. Last I heard, they were saying he'll be okay, but it was a close call. There's an EMT on the side of the house checking him out."

"Let's see how he's doing." Jackson led the way after waving to the other DEA agents huddled together near the fence. "What's the head count so far?"

Cole walked with long strides as he spoke. "Three behind bars, one on the way to the station in cuffs, one in the house with the lieutenant, two critically wounded near the barn and the one you saw in the back of a cruiser. That makes eight."

"That might be all of them, but I'll need a list of names to make sure the members of the ring we know of are all accounted for." Jackson turned when he heard Bailey's voice.

She ran toward them from around the corner of the house. "The lieutenant wants to see you!"

At that moment, a shadow shifted in the distance, and Jackson spotted the glint of a gun.

FIFTEEN

Bailey slowed from a jog to a steady walk, then abruptly stopped and stared. Jackson had whipped his weapon from its holster, his attention laser focused on the darkness across the dirt road. Seconds felt like minutes as her mind took in the events surrounding her. A police officer's flashlight beam exposed the man in the mask, standing beneath a tree branch, glaring at her. Even with his face covered, she recognized him by his build and clothing. This was the man who'd killed Amy and Dr. Daniels.

He lifted the barrel of his gun and aimed it directly at her.

She couldn't move. She couldn't breathe. *God*...

A loud pop shattered the fear-induced silence in her ears. Jackson fired a second round. The shooter who'd haunted her thoughts for the past two days buckled, then fell into the shadows. The police officer holding the flashlight swept the beam over the prone body while a handful of men in blue swarmed the area, guns ready.

A strange noise escaped Bailey's throat when she sucked in a much-needed breath.

Jackson ran toward her. "Are you okay?"

She could only nod and point to the officer removing

the mask from the dead man's face. His open eyes, still looking at her, brought on a nerve-wracking shudder.

"That's Anthony Hill. I recognize him from those surveillance pictures." Jackson slipped his arm protectively around Bailey's shoulders. His comforting touch gave her strength and kept her from dropping to the ground. "Evidently," Jackson continued, "Anthony is more like his father than anyone thought. After years of not getting involved in his father's drug trafficking business, he killed innocent people to keep his sister's new identity a secret."

"Judging by the mask, he wanted to keep his own identity a secret as well," Cole added. "The timing of tonight's events is making more sense now. They sent one man to get the thumb drive and most likely kill the leak from the police department, while Hill brought the rest of his father's organization here to kill the two of you."

"All witnesses would be eliminated at once," Jackson said, his voice grim and his expression dark.

Bailey tensed at the word *eliminated*.

"Let's get you back to the house." Jackson escorted her to the front porch with Cole following behind. The lieutenant stepped outside and greeted them with a scowl.

"We can stop looking for the masked shooter." Cole signaled with a thumb over his shoulder, pointing in the general direction of the body. "Anthony Hill is dead. Jackson took him down before he could kill Bailey."

The lines in the lieutenant's forehead deepened when his gaze fell on Jackson. "Why didn't you tell me you're DEA? I had to hear about it from your associate over there."

Drug Enforcement Administration? Bailey stared

up at the man who had pretended to be a handyman. She'd suspected he might have had some sort of law enforcement training, but she never dreamed he was a federal agent.

He avoided eye contact with her, focusing on the lieutenant.

"We couldn't say anything until the leak in the department was caught," Jackson admitted. "And this was a discussion I had planned to hold in person, behind a closed door, when the time was right."

Cole tried to usher Bailey into the house, but she jerked her arm away from him. "I'm not going anywhere. I have the right to hear this." Jackson had kept a huge secret from her. And secrets always triggered a sense of betrayal, no matter what the circumstance. She needed answers, and time to process.

Jackson's eyes pleaded for her to understand. "This is what I wanted to tell you after we wrapped up the case."

She gestured toward the thug in the back of the cruiser. "Looks to me like we've reached that point. As far as I can see, the men chasing us are either dead, on the way to the hospital or in cuffs."

"Can we speak privately?" Jackson left the lieutenant and Cole behind as he walked toward the tree swing off to the side of the yard, his expression thoughtful.

Bailey followed him but stood an arm's length away, her whirling emotions refusing to settle. "You know how I feel about lies. I want the truth. All of it."

"I did my best to be as honest as I could under the circumstances." He lifted a hand before she could protest. "I know the omission of facts is a lie. I'm guilty as charged on that score, but I couldn't reveal everything and keep you safe. The last time I shared my undercover status with the DEA, the person I told was killed. Her uncle thought she was feeding me information and shot her between the eyes."

She gaped. First, because a woman had suffered a gruesome death; then, because Bailey realized the nightmare they had been living the past few days was a part of Jackson's everyday life. Working undercover among evil people to stop them was the primary focus of his career, as far as she could tell.

"Can you forgive me for not telling you?"

"I can't think about that right now." Bailey shook her head. There was so much here to take in.

"I understand," Jackson said, although she highly doubted it. "I betrayed your trust by not being completely honest. I know that's something we'll have to work through, but I hope that you can see that there are big differences between me and your ex."

They both turned when a dangerous-looking man she'd never seen before strode up to Jackson. "I hate to interrupt, but I wanted you to know we have a guy who decided to talk now that Anthony Hill is dead. He says that the only member of the trafficking ring still out there is Victoria's bodyguard. And he won't leave her side."

Jackson nodded. "Bailey, this is Special Agent Martinez."

The other man gave her a smile. "You've got all of us impressed, Bailey. You might just be the best informant we've had all year. This guy'll probably get promoted to a cushy desk job after this," he said, nudging Jackson.

Jackson grimaced. "She's *not* an informant."

"That came out wrong. What I meant is you didn't need one because Bailey was extremely helpful, like we all hoped she'd be." Uncertainty flashed across the agent's face. "I'll wait with Steele, but don't take too long."

Jackson lifted a finger. "Give me one minute," he told the man, who nodded and walked away.

Bailey had never seen that agent before. Why had he thought she might be helpful? And when? The hesitation on Jackson's face gave her pause. "Was Agent Martinez around this whole time?"

"Not at the beginning." When she narrowed her eyes, he added, "The guy standing next to the police cruiser is his partner. They drove up from Phoenix the night of the shooting."

Bailey glanced over at the third agent—a tall man dressed in jeans and a dark blue hoodie. "They're from Phoenix. So…they could have taken me away from Sedona. To someplace safe. And you didn't let them?"

"I tried, but our supervisor said Martinez and Steele couldn't take responsibility for you because there was no evidence at that time connecting the shooting to our case. That meant the local authorities were responsible for protecting you—except, with the leak to consider, Cole and I didn't trust anyone here. We thought you would be safer with me."

She nodded slowly, still grappling with the details. "And your supervisor was okay with that?"

"Not at first…" Jackson clenched his jaw.

The cloudy haze in her mind lifted, and everything came together with sharp clarity. "Your job was to see if I could connect the dots for you. That's why you asked me all those questions to 'help Cole solve the case so I could go home.' And why you kept telling me you thought the doctor was working with the drug ring.

You let me think I was forcing you to take me along on searches when it's what you really wanted all along. I was such a fool."

"No, you weren't. It's not like that. I didn't care what my supervisor wanted. My top priority was to protect you. I tried to keep you away from those searches because I was falling in love with you, but you had a convincing argument each time, and letting you help meant solving the case faster, which was the only way you'd be safe. Bailey, I did the best I could under the circumstances."

Her heart thudded. She had been falling in love with Jackson, too. She wanted to believe him. But then, she had also wanted to believe Rod. "My former fiancé had a convincing argument the first time I caught him with another woman, and I took him back. That was my mistake—and it's one I promised myself I'd never make again. I don't know what's real right now. You sound convincing, but you kept so much hidden from me, and you lied about your job. I can't be positive you're still not keeping secrets."

"I'm not." Sorrow filled Jackson's eyes. "Bailey…" He stretched his hand out to keep her from walking away, but she stepped out of reach.

Agent Martinez jogged toward them. "Jackson, we know where Victoria's hiding. We have to go *now*. She's flying out of the country *today*."

With a heavy heart, Bailey crossed the yard, heading toward Cole and the lieutenant while the DEA agents ran off. Jackson would capture the kingpin's daughter and earn his promotion, and she would return home to go on with her life. Whatever that might look like.

"Cole, I'd like to go to the police station to give my statement."

The detective glanced at his brother and the other agents running toward their vehicles before offering her a sympathetic smile. "We'll call your father on the way so he can meet you there. Even if Jackson and the others don't catch Victoria and her bodyguard, those two are leaving the country. It's time for you to go home."

Tears born of both joy and sorrow filled her eyes at the same moment Jackson sped down the dirt road in his father's truck, leaving her behind to arrest the kingpin's daughter.

Victoria and her bodyguard were reported to be hiding in a cabin outside Flagstaff. One with sunflowers near the front door. Jackson followed the other agents in his father's truck, glad he didn't have to answer any questions about Bailey. It would have been apparent to everyone back at the ranch that they had argued. And that his relationship with her was anything but professional.

Jackson needed this drive up the mountain freeway to focus his thoughts on the case. Later, he would pray for the right words to say to Bailey to make things right between them again. If she agreed to hear them. *God, please whisper in her ear or soften her heart—whatever it is You do—so she'll talk to me again.*

Regardless of what happened between them, he'd realized that he was ready to move back home to Sedona to be closer to his family. If it turned out the governor really was looking for someone to lead a northern Arizona task force, he'd apply for the position.

It didn't take long to locate the address they'd been

given for Forest Cabin Village. Half a dozen A-frame rentals spread out over a meadow, all sharing the same sand volleyball court and wooden lawn chairs surrounding a stone firepit. Jackson parked near a silver SUV. He wasn't surprised to find only one vehicle. Summer was tourist season in northern Arizona. The mild temperature made it the perfect day for hiking, attending a festival or visiting the Grand Canyon. No one would have any reason to be hanging around the cabins.

After the agents regrouped next to a picnic table, Steele pointed toward the farthest A-frame, which had been built next to the dense forest. "That's the only one with sunflowers."

Jackson had reached back for his gun when the shrill sound of children squealing poured out from a cabin fifty feet away. His gaze jerked toward the SUV and then back to the other agents. From the expression of doubt on their faces, he gathered they shared his assessment. With the only vehicle probably belonging to this family with kids, Victoria was either gone already, had never been here in the first place, or was all alone while her bodyguard ran some errand in their car.

The door to the nearby cabin swung open, and a family of four—all blondes wearing backpacks and carrying water bottles—piled outside. The father unlocked the SUV with a key fob, and the kids, both elementary school–aged girls, climbed inside.

Martinez flashed his badge at the thirtysomething parents. "Have you seen a redheaded woman around here?" He pointed at the cabin with the sunflowers.

Jackson lifted his phone to flash Victoria's post-op picture.

The mother's hazel eyes widened with recognition.

"She took off over an hour ago. I doubt she'll be back. She was yelling at the man with her to hurry up. He practically tossed their bags into the trunk of his convertible and left the key in the drop box."

Jackson gave a silent prayer of thanks for the family's safety. They had no clue how close they had come to danger. "What color was the car, and do you remember what they were wearing?"

The husband's concerned gaze darted over to his giggling children before answering. "The car was white. The man was a big guy with long brown hair and a dark beard. He always wore faded jeans and a black vest over a white T-shirt. He looked like a biker."

"The woman was wearing designer jeans," the wife added. "There's a chance she might be sick. She was bundled up in a pink down jacket with the hood on, even though it wasn't cold outside when they left. Oh, and one more thing. I don't know if it's important or not, but a couple of men stopped by to see them yesterday. They only stayed for a few minutes to drop off a large manila envelope."

Jackson suspected it held fake passports and the tickets to leave the country. They were most likely in a rush to catch their flight, but from which city? They could take a small plane out of Flagstaff or Sedona to either Phoenix or Las Vegas. They might even drive there. A quick check of the cabin might provide a clue.

"We're going to look around," Steele explained, handing the woman his card. "Please continue with your plans for the day. It's highly unlikely that the redhead or her companion will return to the area, but if they do, remain inside your cabin and call us."

She read the card. "Drug Enforcement Administration."

"We'll be finding another place to stay." The man quickly led his wife to the SUV.

In their shoes, Jackson would relocate, too. Once the family drove away, he headed toward the cabin with the sunflowers. Martinez walked beside him, calling in the update to their supervisor while Steele located a contact number for the property owner with his phone.

Remembering what had happened at the last house Victoria had rented, Jackson held up his finger for Martinez to wait. "These people like to blow things up."

They both peered through every window with open blinds and couldn't find any sign of incendiary devices. Jackson drew in a deep breath and turned the doorknob. "It's unlocked."

"Don't just stand there. Open it," Martinez growled, standing thirty feet away.

Jackson, still jittery after surviving his recent bomb encounter, stepped off the porch. "You open it."

A huge grin spread across Martinez's face. "Let's draw sticks. Short one goes in first."

"The owner gave us permission to search the cabin." Steele shoved his phone into his pocket and marched in through the door as if it were no big deal.

When the roof didn't fly off in a fiery explosion, Jackson followed the other agents inside. The aroma of sanitizing chemicals wafted through the air, so strong that it smelled as if the place had been flooded with bleach. "Somehow, I doubt these two are germaphobes. They must have wiped away their prints and destroyed any traces of DNA instead of blowing the place up."

"If only everyone would make that choice." Steele

opened the coat closet, which contained a broom, dust-pan and a box of trash bags.

The sparsely furnished living room reminded Jackson of his friend's college dorm room, where everything had been brown and cheaply constructed. The three split up to conduct their search.

Inside the bathroom, Jackson recognized the smell of hair dye from the times his mother had touched up her roots. He checked the shower, sink, cabinets and tiled floor for any residue but found nothing. Not a single drop of colorant anywhere to let them know her latest hair-color change.

Back in the living room, Martinez planted his hands on his hips. "This was a waste of time."

"I wouldn't say that." Jackson opened the back door. "Victoria hid her hair under the jacket because she colored it this morning." He located the metal trash can behind the cabin and lifted the lid. Empty. *That doesn't make sense.*

He had a difficult time believing the kingpin's daughter would have taken the horrible-smelling bottles in the car with her. She most likely wiped her prints off and tossed them. But where? "Check every trash can around here. We need to know what color her hair is now."

Several minutes later, Martinez reappeared, carrying a white kitchen trash bag and a box of permanent hair dye. "I found this mixed in with the neighbors' garbage."

Jackson reached for the box featuring a brunette model and read, "Warm Sienna."

"The other trash cans are empty," Steele said, jogging over to where Jackson and Martinez stood on either side of a picnic table.

"We might find something else helpful in here." Martinez dumped the bag's contents onto the flat wooden surface. A handful of sanitizing wipes landed on top of a pile of fast-food containers.

Steele held up a box of colored contacts. "Victoria— or whatever name she is going by—now has blue eyes."

"And loves Uncle Mel's." Martinez held up one of a dozen fast-food cups with matching chicken logos. "By the looks of these wrappers, they must have eaten there for breakfast, lunch and dinner."

Jackson only knew of one Uncle Mel's. It was located a block away from Bailey's house.

The hairs on the back of his neck stood on end. "I think they've gone after Bailey."

Steele furrowed his brow. "You got that from a soda cup?"

"They wouldn't drive from Flagstaff to Sedona for Mel's chicken every day unless they were watching her house, waiting for her to come home."

The other agent still looked confused. "Why not just kidnap Bailey's father and force her to give herself up in exchange?"

"The police would have found out and set a trap," Martinez explained. "She was with Jackson, whose brother is the detective, remember?" He scooped the garbage into a trash can and continued, "Jackson, call Cole and see if he can meet you at Bailey's house. I don't think Victoria has a reason to stick around a minute longer than necessary, but I could be wrong."

Steele nodded. "Martinez and I will head over to the Sedona airport to see if Victoria took a small plane out of there. She's got good reason to leave. Last night's shooting made the morning news. By now, she knows there's no one here with any clout to help her if she runs into trouble."

"But she also knows her brother is dead," Jackson replied grimly. "And that might be reason enough for her to want to personally tie up one last loose end before she goes."

SIXTEEN

After signing her statement at the police department, Bailey stood in front of Cole's desk, clutching her newly returned purse and phone to her chest. She felt almost normal, holding her personal belongings once again.

"Cole, thank you for everything you did to help end this nightmare. I wish…" She tried to find the right words to describe how she'd wanted things to go—but she couldn't manage to string them together. Maybe because she still wasn't entirely sure herself. She wasn't happy with how things had ended, but at the same time, she didn't see any other way they could have gone.

"I think I understand." He ran a hand across his forehead. "It's none of my business, but you should know Jackson's feelings for you are real—and obvious to our entire family." When she lowered her gaze instead of responding, Cole offered his hand. "It was a pleasure to meet you, Bailey Scott. Take care of yourself."

"You, too." She sent him a gentle smile and shook his hand.

Cole was a good man. She would miss him, his family and, most of all, Jackson. After all they had been through together, it didn't seem right to end their relationship this way. She stepped out of the detective's office and headed down the hall, feeling like she'd lost a vital, irreplaceable part of her life.

When her father pushed out of his chair in the waiting area and charged across the room to greet her, Bailey lost her composure. "Dad." She threw her arms around him and sobbed into his chest the way she had when she was a child. "I can't believe you're here and I can finally go home."

Minutes later, her crying slowed to a sniffle, and he stepped back to look her over. "Unless I'm missing something, you managed to make it out of this mess in one piece."

"Physically, yes. I can't say the same emotionally." The events of the past few days had been a never-ending roller coaster. Up—safe for now. Down—death staring her in the face. Up—falling in love. Down—feeling used.

"You can tell me all about it after you've rested." His tone was reassuring but his expression wary. "Let's head home."

"Home." Repeating the word warmed her heart and released the top layer of tension. "I can now relate to Dorothy in *The Wizard of Oz*."

"I can relate to her uncle at the end of the movie." He opened the police station door for her. "I'm relieved to have you safely back where you belong."

As Bailey eased into the passenger seat of her father's car, she was struck by how nothing had changed. The radio was set to his favorite country-western station; coins filled one cupholder, with a Maryland-state quarter on top; and a rolled-up gum wrapper rested in the same corner of the dashboard. She found it both comforting and…odd.

With the sun rising above the horizon, she turned her focus to God's bright array of colors and settled in for the drive home. Every few minutes, she reached out and touched her father's arm to make sure she wasn't dreaming. Each time, he sent her a warm smile.

"Here we are," he said in a light singsong voice as he pulled into the driveway and parked. "Home sweet home."

Instead of jumping out and rushing inside the way she'd pictured this moment a hundred times over the past few days, she sat still, studying the older creamy beige–colored house surrounded by desert willow trees and yellow bird-of-paradise bushes. Once again, she found it strange that everything looked the same. While she'd been running for her life, with Jackson at her side, the world she left behind hadn't changed—but she had.

Keys in hand, her father turned to her, the lines in his forehead deepening with concern. "Something wrong?"

"No. I was just thinking." She waved away her thoughts and unlocked the car door. "Don't mind me. Let's go in."

"You sure you don't want to sit here a bit longer and talk? For a minute there, your mind looked a million miles away." He waited for her to choose her next move.

After a slight hesitation, she leaned back against the seat's headrest. "When we pulled up to the house, I noticed it looks exactly the way it did when I left for work Saturday morning…"

"And it didn't feel right because your whole life had just turned upside down." When she slowly nodded, he went on, "I had a similar experience after your mother left. Everything around me seemed so small and meaningless compared to my all-encompassing pain."

A tear slid down her cheek and dropped onto her hands clutched in her lap. "I used to think Mom abandoning us hadn't affected me because you were always there—but it did. I realized that, because of her, I had unconsciously kept most people at arm's length, not wanting to get hurt."

"Then Rod walked into your life, and you thought you were ready to give love a chance." His voice cracked. "I wish I could have seen through him and saved you that grief."

She shook her head. "I'm the one who should have seen through him. But I let him fool me. Let him make me powerless. And that was why I swore no one would ever trample over my heart again."

"And now?"

"Now I know what happened to me then was nothing compared to running away from murderers." A slight chuckle escaped her lips. "It sounds cliché, but life is too short. I'm going to do those things I had been putting off. Take ceramics classes, learn a new language and how to ice skate." She almost said something about getting back in to horseback riding, but the thought reminded her of Jackson. "And travel. The two of us."

He smiled, but it fell short of reaching his eyes.

"Don't you want to travel? We could go to Italy and see the ruins."

"It's not that." A wave of apprehension crossed his face. "You should travel the world with your husband—after you meet the right guy. I know it doesn't seem possible right now, but he's out there, and you'll find him, one day."

Her stomach twisted into a knot. Maybe having a deep discussion with her father wasn't a good idea after all. "I was speaking about living, not about falling in love. That will take time, which isn't a problem. I'm happy living here with you."

He scrubbed a hand over his cheek. "Don't get me wrong. I appreciate your help, and I enjoy having your company, but I would hate to think you were passing up a family of your own to look after me."

All this time, she had prayed to come home and… "You don't want me to help you?" Even she could hear the hurt in her voice. Her mother had left her, and now her father didn't want her?

"Honey, I love having you here, but I want more for you—when the time is right. And it never will be if you don't allow yourself to come to peace with the past. You need to forgive yourself and those who hurt you."

Her limbs felt heavy with fatigue. He was right. She had layers of trust issues, starting with her mother, then shellacked into place thanks to her former fiancé and now Jackson. She wanted to heal. "What do you suggest?"

"I'm no therapist," her father said, "but I watch them on television. They ask a lot of questions. How hard can that be?" When she shrugged, he continued, "Okay, let's start with this one. What is your first thought when I say you should forgive yourself for staying with Rod?"

"My first thought…" She reached inside for an honest answer. "If I forgive myself, I might forget, and then I'll trust the wrong person again." *Which I already did.*

Her father nodded while he contemplated his next question. "Did you suspect Rod was cheating?"

"Yes." That answer was an easy one. "I had my suspicions all along. I should never have stayed with him after the first time I caught him, but I fell for his excuse. Now I know better."

Her father's next question surprised her. "Would God have given Rod a second chance?"

God? She faltered, and it took her a long moment to answer. "Yeah, He would have. So me giving Rod time to prove himself wasn't foolish after all?"

Her father shook his head. "If you hadn't, you would have always wondered. You loved him—or at least, you thought you did. If you'd let him go early on, you might have regretted it later. Now you know who he truly was—and proved that your instincts are solid. You can trust them as you navigate the world and meet new people."

"As long as I keep an eye on my credit cards."

He chuckled. "And after you put one of those tracking apps on our phones. And carry yours with you at all times. I never want to lose you again."

Bailey gave him a big hug and then climbed out of the passenger seat. Her father's question about God gave her a whole new perspective. Knowing she wasn't foolish for giving Rod another chance made her feel so much better about that situation. She was ready to forgive him and her mother. And herself.

Now for the tough one: Jackson. She'd been too emotional when they last spoke, and she hadn't treated him fairly. If he ever wanted to see her again, she'd listen with an open mind. In the meantime, she intended to pray and hand her troubles over to God. He would let her know if she should give Jackson another chance. If he wanted one.

Inside the house, Bailey installed the GPS app on

their phones, just like her dad had wanted. Then she changed into sweatpants and a pink top before curling up on the living room sofa next to her father. She tried to focus on the antiques show he was watching—much too loudly for her liking—but her eyelids wouldn't stay open. "Dad, I need a nap."

He kissed her forehead. "Make it a long one. I doubt you've slept much lately."

"You're right about that." She slipped her phone into the pocket of her pants, then trudged down the hall with the sound of the television filling the house. Inside her room, she closed the door, ready to fall into bed. The open window caught her eye. *Wait, I didn't—*

Before she could finish her thought, a muscular man swooped out of the closet. He swiftly grabbed her with one arm around her waist and the other hand pressing a sweet-smelling cloth over her nose and mouth. She struggled to scream and escape but to no avail. He held her tight against his massive chest for what seemed like an eternity while her bare feet kicking against the carpet grew weaker. Eventually, her mind turned foggy, and the room faded to black.

Back at the cabins, Jackson tried phoning Cole and grew aggravated when he kept getting sent to voice mail. "Call me right away. My gut says Victoria and her bodyguard may be after Bailey. I don't have her number, her father is unlisted and I don't know how to reach her. Please warn Bailey and meet me at her house."

He threw open the truck door, jumped in and sped away. Winding switchbacks slowed his progress down the mountain, but it was still the shortest route. His thumb tapped against the steering wheel with nervous energy each time he had to press on the brake. When the pine trees of the national forest gave way to red rock formations without him hearing from his brother, Jackson's patience wore thin. What was taking Cole so long to call?

An hour had passed by the time Jackson reached Bailey's neighborhood. His gaze darted from left to right, ahead through the windshield and over to the rearview mirror. No sign of danger…yet.

At her house, he repeatedly pressed the doorbell while holding his badge up to the peephole.

An older gentleman answered with more than a touch of annoyance in his voice. "What now? We've already told the police everything we know."

Jackson flashed his badge once more. "I'm Special Agent Walker. Is Bailey here? It's vitally important I see her. She may still be in danger."

"Oh, Lord, no." He swung open the door and stepped aside. "I'm her father. Come on in. I'll wake her."

If this had been a social call, Jackson would have waited in the living room, but he had to know she was safe. He followed Mr. Scott down the hallway, making sure to stay three feet behind to give Bailey privacy.

When she didn't answer the knock, Mr. Scott cracked the door open before pushing it against the wall. "Bailey?"

The panic in the man's voice propelled Jackson into action. With his pulse racing, he rushed inside and found the window wide open. Bailey was nowhere in sight.

Mr. Scott checked the closet. "Maybe she's in the bathroom. I've been home the whole time, watching TV. She could *not* have left without me seeing her."

Jackson leaned over the windowsill and confirmed his suspicions. The missing screen was propped up against the house, and footprints in the red dirt led toward the backyard's open gate. *No!* What he'd feared the most was playing out before his very eyes despite every attempt he'd made to keep Bailey safe.

"They have her." Jackson placed both hands on Mr. Scott's shoulders. "Call the police," he instructed, forcing his voice to remain calm. "Tell them she's been kidnapped. And if you hear anything from Bailey, or her abductors, call me right away."

The color drained from the distraught man's face.

Jackson grabbed a notepad from a small desk in the corner and scribbled out his phone number. "What was she wearing when you last saw her?"

"Um." Mr. Scott scrubbed his hands over his forehead. "Gray sweatpants and a pink shirt."

Hoping Martinez and Steele had a lead on Victoria and her bodyguard, Jackson bolted out of the bedroom and down the hall. He'd check in with the others once he was in the truck.

Before he could cross the living room, Mr. Scott called out to him.

"Bailey's phone. It's not here. If she has it, we can find her."

"What?" Jackson spun around and watched the man grab a smartphone from the coffee table.

"I insisted she install this GPS app after she came home. I never wanted to lose track of her again." He pressed an image on the screen and handed over the phone.

Hope took root as Jackson pressed the link labeled

Bailey. "It says she's here." He handed the phone back to her father. "Call her number."

Seconds later, while walking through the dining room, Jackson heard a faint ringing float in from outside. He removed the bar securing the sliding glass door and yanked it open. The sound grew louder.

His search ended at the open backyard gate, where he found her phone on the ground beside a metal fence post. The word *Dad* flashed across the screen as the caller. Jackson grabbed the device and peered over the fence. No vehicles.

Her father quickly reached his side, holding up his phone. "There's another—"

Jackson stormed into the alley, where he found fresh tire marks. They'd driven off with Bailey in the car. Tamping down his erratic emotions, he pushed the phone into her father's free hand. "Can you check to see if she took any pictures or sent any text messages? Anything that might help us find her?"

"I've been trying to tell you I also bought those little round discs. You know, the ones that tell you where you left your keys or backpack? She promised to always carry one with her, at least until I felt better. I believed at the time that I was acting paranoid, but…" He handed over his phone.

"You are brilliant." Jackson opened the other app and located Bailey—or rather, the tracking disc—heading toward Phoenix. His mood soared.

"Bring my daughter home," Mr. Scott pleaded.

"I will, or die trying. I promise." Jackson ran from the house as Cole pulled up to the curb and climbed out of his car.

Jackson rushed over to join him, pushing him back

down into the driver's seat. "They have Bailey! They're heading toward Phoenix on the interstate." Jackson rushed around to hop in on the passenger side. "You have a siren."

Cole called it in, and the lieutenant said they would track his progress with GPS and pass on any updates to the appropriate law enforcement agencies, including the DEA.

With Jackson acting as navigator in the passenger seat, Cole sped through town and over the state road to the I-17 freeway, where they drove down the mountain. "Where are they now?"

"New River Road. The road they're on leads to Lake Pleasant." Jackson furrowed his brow, his mind racing through the information he'd reviewed so many times in the files that connected the traffickers to the area. He glanced over at his brother. "Doctor Daniels has a boat there. Maybe they do, too."

"Or they're planning to hide out in his." Once they exited onto the dirt road, close enough to require extreme caution, Cole flipped off the siren and slowed to a speed closer to the posted limit. Before long, the calm blue waters of the lake appeared in the distance—an oasis springing out of the desert. "Do we know what type of craft we're looking for?"

Jackson took in the rows of boats docked at the marina. "I have no clue. It's a good thing we have the tracker." They entered the parking lot, and he studied Mr. Scott's phone. "According to the app, she's over there." He pointed in the same direction as the arrow on the screen. "I don't see anyone on the walkway."

Jackson led the way as they raced down a long series of steps. Sweat beaded on his forehead beneath his Stetson.

"Ten more feet," Jackson said, checking the screen in his hand. Seconds later, he stopped short of the water's edge. "Something's wrong. Bailey is supposed to be here, but she's not."

They both leaned over the railing, scanning the dirt and weeds. Then, remembering a video detailing this type of tracker's functions, Jackson used Mr. Scott's phone to activate the audio signal.

The brothers followed the beeping sound to a clump of weeds off to the side of the steps. Cole reached over and pulled out the black-and-white disc. It was cracked but still functional. "I'm guessing Victoria's bodyguard found it."

"Or it fell out of her pocket." Jackson drew in a grounding breath and tucked one side of his shirt into his pants, providing easy access to the Glock in his waist holster. "She has to be here somewhere. Let's find her." Resisting the urge to call out her name, he hurried forward down the steps and across the walkway to the docks. *God, please help us save Bailey.*

Moving as quietly as possible, they listened and scanned every watercraft docked along their path. Most were empty motorboats. They were fortunate it wasn't a busier weekend.

While searching another aisle of boats, a glassy object lying on a wooden plank up ahead caught Jackson's eye. Drawing closer, he recognized Bailey's necklace, the one she always clung to when she needed comfort or thought of home. The clear triangular magnifying pendant reflected the sun's rays. The chain's silver clasp was broken. Either someone had yanked it off her or she'd left it as a marker for him.

Jackson lifted a finger to his lips to signal for quiet before he pointed to the cabin cruiser closest to the piece of jewelry. Before he could step aboard, a bearded man in jeans and a black vest over a white T-shirt stepped out the cabin door. He spotted them and grabbed for the gun at his waist.

Cole and Jackson both fired shots at the same time. The bodyguard stumbled and fell overboard with a splash, alerting whoever else was on board.

The cabin door swung open again. Victoria slid out with a gun held on Bailey, whose wide eyes were filled with fear and locked on Jackson's. Duct tape covered her mouth, and her hands were tied in front of her with rope, which explained how she could have pulled her necklace off and leave it behind for him.

Jackson forced his mind to focus on Victoria, the predator here. He couldn't let his judgment be affected by his feelings for Bailey.

Sirens sounded in the distance. They were still too far to be of much help.

The kingpin's daughter held Bailey by her upper arm. "Drop your guns, or she's dead."

"We can't do that," Cole answered matter-of-factly. "And if you kill her, we'll shoot you."

Victoria appeared to mull over that piece of information. "Then stay back and untie the boat. If you do as I say, I'll leave her unharmed once I get where I'm going."

Jackson glanced at his brother before complying. The unspoken message was to shoot when possible. He tossed the end of the rope onto the boat. "This is a lake. You won't get far."

"I will as long as I have your girlfriend." Victoria sneered, her hate radiating off her body in waves. "That's right. I heard all about you two lovebirds and what happened at your lousy ranch. I knew then that she would be my insurance policy. Keep your agents away from me and she lives."

"Her father's men all have the same lawyer," Cole explained. "He paid a visit to the jail this morning."

"They told him you murdered my brother in cold blood." Victoria pulled Bailey closer. "So if you think I'm not up to doling out a little pain to your side, think again. Now, stay back, or I'll shoot her foot, then her arm, then—"

Bailey closed her eyes, dropped her head forward and then snapped it back against Victoria's face. Victoria screamed and reached for her bloody nose at the same time her captive rushed to the edge of the boat and jumped overboard.

Cole shot twice. Jackson dove into the cold water after Bailey, who was still tied up.

His pulse surged when he located her deep below the surface, and he swept her up with one hand around her waist. He kicked hard, carrying her up toward the air where the sun's rays glinted off the water.

They dragged in deep breaths before he swam to the dock, holding her close. Cole reached out to pull Bailey up onto the wooden planks. Once she was safely on the walkway, Jackson climbed up and noticed the extra gun tucked into his brother's waist, presumably the one belonging to Victoria.

"Is she alive?" Jackson asked, his breathing labored as he worked at the binds securing Bailey's wrists, trying to free her. Her eyes pleaded for him to hurry.

"Victoria's alive but unconscious." The sirens grew louder as Cole called in an update to the local police.

Water dripped from Bailey's hair onto her soaking-wet clothing, and she shivered from head to toe. The blazing sun would soon warm her skin and dry her off, but she had to be uncomfortable at the moment, and he was desperate to make things better for her.

Jackson dropped the rope once he freed her, then removed the tape from her mouth with one quick tug, hoping it would hurt less that way.

Bailey rubbed at her face and worked her jaw. "I knew you'd find me." She threw her arms around him. "I'm sorry I got so angry at the ranch."

She shuddered, and he held her close. He thanked God she was alive and relatively unharmed. "I love you, Bailey. I think I have from the moment I first laid eyes on you."

"I love you, too. When I thought I was going to die, I wanted nothing more than to be with you and tell you how much you mean to me."

The dock vibrated as half a dozen local officers swarmed the marina. Their boots thudded over the planks as a security guard pointed them in the direction of the boat and toward the bodyguard trying to swim away, despite his gunshot wounds.

A sense of urgency forced Jackson to speak faster. "I was scared to death of losing you." He pressed a gentle kiss to her soft lips and then locked his gaze on hers. "I'll have to leave for Texas soon, but I'll come back as often as I can. We'll find a way to make this work."

She rested her head back against his chest. "I know we can. God will help us find the way."

EPILOGUE

Bailey sat in her living room, waiting for Jackson to arrive while cuddling her kitten. The same one he'd saved when he opened the door of Victoria's rental home—right before it exploded. He'd made repeated trips to the lot surrounding the scorched remains until he found the shy feline hopping over a burnt piece of wood. They named her Phoenix after the mythical bird that rose from the ashes. That was six months ago. So much had happened since then.

Jackson was true to his word and flew back from Texas almost every weekend while the DEA wrapped up the case against the trafficking ring. Interpol found Dante Hill hiding in France along with the few remaining members of the trafficking ring. Several had pleaded guilty to reduced charges, but even with the plea bargains, most of them would still spend decades in prison. As would Victoria.

During this time, Bailey and Jackson had enjoyed the chance to date like ordinary people who never felt the need to hide in the back of a florist's van or in the trunk of a car. Every minute they spent together, they grew closer.

Jackson had been thrilled to accept a position supervising a northern Arizona drug task force that had him moving back to his home state. He didn't mind the commutes to Flagstaff, and she was relieved he didn't have to work undercover. His job still held dangers, but she knew they both appreciated that he no longer had to hide so much of himself away.

Her cell phone rang. She was surprised to see her father was calling. "Hi! How are you and Uncle Sid settling into your new house?"

"You wouldn't believe this place. Did I tell you it has three pools and two golf courses?"

A smile spread across her face. "I was there for the tour, remember?"

"That's right, but it's even better when you're here to enjoy it. Sid and I are taking Italian cooking classes at the community center tonight."

"I thought you two were eating in the dining hall?"

"We are, but Sid has a thing for one of the ladies in the class."

Bailey smiled, happy her father and his brother had chosen to combine their resources to enjoy their golden years in an active retirement community. "And what about you? Have you met any nice women?"

"A couple, but I'm more selective than Sid." His voice sounded jovial, and it did her heart good. "I think I'll try the pottery class next."

"I can't wait to see your first project." Bailey ran her hand over Phoenix's fur. "Jackson and I will drive up to Flagstaff to visit you next weekend."

"That's great. I look forward to seeing you both. So, how's work?"

"Busy, but good." Bailey had accepted a job offer

from the pediatrician who attended her church a month after the funerals for Dr. Daniels and Amy. She was hesitant to work as a bookkeeper in the medical field again, but on the other hand, she had bills to pay. Before long, she was checking the appointment schedule in the mornings and making a point to keep her office door open whenever the babies came in for well checkups. She couldn't help but wonder what it would be like to have one of her own.

She heard the hum of an engine and carried the kitten to the living room window. "I need to go now, Dad. Jackson just pulled into the drive."

"Give him my best."

"I will." Bailey lowered Phoenix to the area rug and swatted away the hair left behind on her black slacks. By the time she was fur free, the bell had rung, and she swung the door open. Her insides warmed every time she gazed up at Jackson's handsome face. "I'm so glad you're here. I'm starved."

He grinned. "Is that the only reason you're happy to see me?"

"No, but it's a big one." She leaned in for a quick, sweet kiss, followed by one that lingered a bit longer. "Where are you taking me?"

"On a picnic. Ready?"

"Let me grab my jacket."

During their drive to the ranch in his new truck, she glanced over at him. He was everything she had always hoped for in a boyfriend: caring, understanding, willing to discuss feelings. That last thought made her smile. He was a rare breed of man—and a particularly good-looking one, at that.

Jackson entered through the back gate and turned

down a dirt road she'd never traveled over before. Soon, he parked on a cleared lot. He grinned at her. "Let's get out."

Bailey slipped out of her seat and pushed the door shut. "Are your parents building something here?"

"In due time." He removed a picnic basket from the back seat and handed it to her. Next, he pulled a folding table and two chairs from the back of the truck and assembled them on the red dirt for their picnic.

Surprised and delighted, she watched him work. When he was finished, she placed the basket on one of the chairs. Then he handed her a white tablecloth. "Would you do the honor, please?"

"Of course." After she covered the table, he placed two candles in crystal holders on top of the flat surface and lit the wicks. She admired the scene, which was like it had been cut right out of a romantic movie. "Are we celebrating something?"

"We are." Still standing, Jackson took her hands in his. "What do you think about all of this?"

"It's amazing. Romantic." The clearing captured her attention once again. "Now, will you tell me what this land was cleared for?"

He dropped a kiss on her forehead. "Our house."

She blinked rapidly. "'Our house'?"

"If you'll have me." Jackson removed a diamond ring from his jeans pocket and held it up for her to see the brilliantly shining stone in the afternoon sun before he lowered himself down to one knee. "Bailey Scott, will you do me the honor of being my wife?"

She covered her open mouth with both hands before answering, "Yes, yes, yes."

"Are you sure, now?" he teased, returning to his feet to slip the ring on her finger.

"A million times, yes." She threw her arms around his neck. "I never knew it was possible to love someone this much."

"I love you, too." He pressed a kiss to her lips that said he would be hers forever. "I thank God every day for bringing you into my life."

Bailey smiled up at him. "And I thank God for everything He still has planned for us."

* * * * *

Dear Reader,

Thank you for reading my first Love Inspired Suspense novel. This experience has been a dream come true. Looking back, I can see God planned the perfect time for my adventure to begin. In Jackson and Bailey's story, their high-stakes adventure takes them through Sedona, my favorite place in Arizona. God's work is evident in the beautiful red rock formations surrounding them and in their spiritual journey. Jackson's connection to God had waned while working around vicious criminals. Now, with Bailey's influence, he's praying again. She learns to forgive herself and others for past mistakes. Together, their faith grows as well as their relationship. I hope you see God's work in your life, too.

I love to stay connected with readers. You can join my newsletter at authorTinaWheeler.com or on Facebook or Twitter to learn more about me and my books.

Blessings,
Tina Wheeler

COMING NEXT MONTH FROM
Love Inspired Suspense

ALASKAN AVALANCHE ESCAPE
K-9 Search and Rescue • by Darlene L. Turner

After discovering someone is deliberately triggering avalanches, mountain survival expert Jayla Hoyt and her K-9 set out to stop the culprit—but he sets his sights on them. Can she and Alaska park ranger Bryson Clarke catch the criminal before they all lose their lives?

GUARDING HIS CHILD
by Karen Kirst

Following her best friend's gruesome murder, Deputy Skye Saddler is assigned to protect the victim's baby and the father who didn't know the little girl existed. Now that rancher Nash Wilder is the killer's next target, keeping close to Skye is their best chance at survival.

DETECTING SECRETS
Deputies of Anderson County • by Sami A. Abrams

When pregnant teens and babies go missing, Sheriff Dennis Monroe works with marriage and family therapist Charlotte Bradley and her air-scent dog to put an end to a black-market baby smuggling ring in Anderson County. But when the kidnapper's scheme includes Charlotte, can she rely on Dennis to protect her?

PERILOUS SECURITY DETAIL
Honor Protection Specialists • by Elizabeth Goddard

When bodyguard Everly Honor rescues her secretive ex-boyfriend from an intentional hit-and-run, he hires her to guard his niece. But with danger closing in on all sides, Sawyer Blackwood must reveal hidden truths...or put their lives at risk.

DEADLY VENGEANCE
by Jodie Bailey

Someone wants profiler Gabe Buchanan dead, and he has no idea why. When his identity is wiped clean, he's forced to trust military investigator Hannah Austin, the woman who hurt him in the past, to restore his life. As deadly threats escalate, they'll have to find the culprit before it's too late.

THEME PARK ABDUCTION
by Patsy Conway

A cartel kidnaps Rebecca Salmon's son off a roller coaster, and now she needs help from FBI agent Jake Foster to solve a series of clues planted throughout the theme park. As they race against time and evade henchmen gunning for them, will Jake's secrets get in the way of saving her son?

_____

LOOK FOR THESE AND OTHER LOVE INSPIRED BOOKS WHEREVER BOOKS ARE SOLD, INCLUDING MOST BOOKSTORES, SUPERMARKETS, DISCOUNT STORES AND DRUGSTORES.

LISCNM0123

Get 4 FREE REWARDS!

We'll send you 2 FREE Books plus 2 FREE Mystery Gifts.

FREE
Value Over
$20

Both the **Love Inspired®** and **Love Inspired® Suspense** series feature compelling novels filled with inspirational romance, faith, forgiveness and hope.

HARLEQUIN
PLUS

Announcing a **BRAND-NEW**
multimedia subscription service
for romance fans like you!

Read, Watch and Play.

Experience the easiest way to get
the romance content you crave.

Start your **FREE 7 DAY TRIAL** at
<u>www.harlequinplus.com/freetrial</u>.